That We May Live

That We May Live

Speculative Chinese Fiction

CALICO

"Lip Service" is from Issue 1 of *Chinese Arts and Literature*, published by Xanadu Press, 2017.

"Flourishing Beasts" is from *Strange Beasts of China* and published with permission from Tilted Axis Press.

That We May Live is first in the Calico Series.

Two Lines Press
582 Market Street, Suite 700, San Francisco, CA 94104
www.twolinespress.com

ISBN: 978-1-949641-00-4

Cover design by Crisis
Typesetting and interior design by LOKI

Printed in the United States of America

Library of Congress Cataloging-in-Publication Data

TITLE: That we may live : speculative Chinese fiction.
DESCRIPTION: San Francisco, CA : Two Lines Press, [2020] | Series: Calico Series | Summary: "An approachable introduction to contemporary speculative fiction from mainland China and Hong Kong that touches on issues of urbanization, sexuality, and propaganda"-- Provided by publisher.
IDENTIFIERS: LCCN 2019041416 | ISBN 9781949641004 (paperback)
SUBJECTS: LCSH: Short stories, Chinese--Translations into English. | Chinese fiction--21st century--Translations into English. | Science fiction, Chinese--Translations into English. | Fantasy fiction, Chinese--Translations into English. | Speculative fiction, Chinese--Translations into English. | Short stories, Chinese--21st century--Translations into English.
CLASSIFICATION: LCC PL2658.E8 T47 2020 | DDC 895.13/0108--dc23
LC record available at https://lccn.loc.gov/2019041416

THIS BOOK WAS PUBLISHED WITH SUPPORT FROM THE NATIONAL ENDOWMENT FOR THE ARTS

Sour Meat

肉變

Dorothy Tse
Translated by Natascha Bruce

有時，F則覺得自己是一灘電油，只要一點點火光，就能把她像一個平原那樣燃燒起來。

"Sometimes she felt like an oil slick, like all she needed was a tiny spark and she'd roar into flames."

Jesus took Mary Magdalene to the mountaintop, where he pulled a woman out of his side and engaged in sexual intercourse with her, swallowing his own semen. Jesus said, "Thus must we do, that we may live."

—"The Greater Questions of Mary," from Epiphanius's *Panarion*

THE TRAIN WAS STILL RACING ALONG ITS TRACKS, SQUEALing as it rounded each bend. F started awake. Was she there yet?

In the seat opposite her was a stiff, unfamiliar silhouette. The woman from earlier was gone, along with the little girl sitting next to her. Now there was a man, with a suitcase wedged into the place beside him. An enormous, battered nylon suitcase, which took up the whole seat and jutted angrily into the aisle.

The train entered a tunnel and the train car shook violently from side to side. The man's dark outline rocked with it.

F took a small ball of crumpled paper from her suit pocket. Something was written on it, but the blue ink of the handwriting had smudged beyond all recognition. A neon-green name flashed up on the train's electronic display, announcing the next stop. Could this be Grandma's town?

F had no way of knowing. Her mother had mentioned the place a number of times, but whenever she talked about Grandma she spoke in their hometown dialect, an unspellable, bubble-like language.

Why was she suddenly so keen to go and see Grandma anyway? She was supposed to be on a different train, to a different town, for a work assignment. She was usually so conscientious; so strict with herself about never making mistakes. What had induced her to make this rash, irresponsible decision? She thought of her mother, trotting out the same old warnings to her every time she left the house, no matter that she was a grown woman now, well into her forties: *Don't talk to strangers. Stick to main roads. Go off the rails and you're done for.* Maybe there was some wisdom to them, after all.

Only a little while before, she had still been sitting on a platform. A long ride on a different train had deposited her in a remote small-town station, where she had waited for her connection. Unfamiliar with the region, she had compulsively checked the display screen overhead, confirming and re-confirming her train number and destination. There was half an hour to wait. She decided she could afford to relax a bit and took a thermos flask of home-brewed tea from her suitcase, only to find herself hesitating over whether to open it. Then she felt a warm, womanly body press against her.

She hadn't noticed the woman sit down. All the stone benches on the platform were two-seaters, which is to say only really wide enough for one person, or a couple snuggled closely together. It was a gloomy afternoon, and a strong scent of sodden grass mingled with the rust on the platform, masking any smell of humans. But very few people were waiting for a train, and all the other benches were empty. Why hadn't the woman gone to sit on one of those?

Was it the tea? It had an intensely sour odor, even from a distance, one F knew could smell a little like vomit—that was why she had waited until she was off the train to bring out the thermos. With the woman there, she wouldn't be able to enjoy it. F glanced at her. She was wearing a cloche hat with a bow on it. It was a bright, jewel-like red, the exact same color as the old, pilled fabric of her long red dress. She certainly stood out, although the hat meant that F couldn't get a proper look at her face.

F turned to a billboard straight ahead, advertising some kind of stimulant drink. She saw the two of them reflected in the glass. Then she noticed a third person—a little girl sitting on the floor (the woman's daughter? her younger sister?) tugging insistently on the woman's flesh-colored stockings. It looked like the girl was pulling on her skin. The woman leaned toward her, waggling her fingers as though to say, "They're coming to get you! They're coming to eat you up!"

Out loud, neither the woman nor the girl said anything at all. Every so often one or the other of them would laugh breezily, while F's reflection stayed sitting deadly serious beside them, as if awaiting inspection.

F was not someone who generally enjoyed staring into mirrors, but she found herself transfixed by her ridiculous reflection in the billboard glass. Her wide, round face was almost completely concealed behind a pair of thick-framed glasses—the same kind she'd been wearing since primary school, despite being only very slightly nearsighted. She had black, straight hair that she never really bothered to style, with bangs that hung stiffly over her eyebrows. Her suit was too big and a little shabby, like something off a secondhand rack. It was the look she'd been aiming for. Grasping, ambitious men were everywhere in her industry, desperate for an opportunity to knock her down, and she had decided it was best to keep her body under wraps. And yet, even shrouded in thick clothes, the body of the woman beside her exuded a powerful, undeniable meatiness. Her disturbing red seemed to be declaring war on everyone around her. "Hey!" it yelled. "Over here! Look at me!"

She couldn't decide whether to get up and move with her luggage to a different spot. The woman shifted closer. F could sense her eyeing the thermos.

"Sorry about the smell," she said, having endured the silence long enough. "I know it can be hard to take."

The woman looked up, but all F could see beneath her hat was a pair of brilliant red lips. They flickered slightly at the corners, as though undergoing a series of mild electric shocks. The little girl looked up too. Her eyes narrowed to slits and she brought both hands in front of her face, waggling her fingers like an animal. Before F could wonder which kind, the woman had snatched the flask from her hands and helped herself to a large gulp.

She has no idea how strong it is, thought F. There had been no time to stop her. But somehow the woman didn't seem affected.

"I knew that's what it was!" she exclaimed. "I'd recognize that smell anywhere."

Recognize that smell? The tea (F insisted on referring to the mysterious drink as tea) was a secret family recipe. Was it possible that the woman knew Grandma?

F's memories of Grandma were hazy. If it hadn't been for the intense, distinctive smell of the tea, she'd have written them off as figments of her imagination. But every so often there would come a moment like this one, talking to the woman at the station, when she had the feeling that the bond between her and Grandma was stronger and more powerful than any she had experienced with other people; that all she had to do was tug on the right thread and all those buried memories and emotions would come flooding back.

But it had been years. F had always known Grandma's tiny town was only a few hours away, and yet she'd never gone to visit. It wasn't only Grandma: aside from her mother, who lived with her, F hardly thought of her family at all. That was just life for city office workers, she reasoned. Did that mean the companies were to blame, because they kept piling on work until nobody had free time for anything else? Then again, F always made sure she had time to keep abreast of the latest news and developments relating to exercise products, especially about the exercise bar repped by her department.

Wanna make your muscles really pop?

For a period, F's dreams had been haunted by the gleaming muscleman from the Power Rod advertisement, racing around with a bar grasped in both hands (*Power Rod* being the name F's colleagues had come up with for the exercise bar). She couldn't use the bar the same way her colleagues did—every so often she would play a part in her own dream, and the muscleman would press it so hard against her throat that she couldn't breathe or cry out.

Even so, whenever her colleagues made dirty jokes about the Power Rod, about the length of a new model, say, or its function and color, F would laugh along with them. These fits of laughter blew past her like hurricanes, hurling debris into the air and sweeping her along with it, causing her to become entangled in matters that had nothing to do with her. Once entangled, she had no power to extricate herself, but neither could she find a way to embrace them fully.

Occasionally F would dream of Grandma, although she would never see her, only hear her voice. Every year, Grandma would find someone from her tiny town to bring F and her mother a couple of bottles of her homemade brew. All kinds of women turned up on their doorstep. F had no idea who they were, and her mother didn't seem to recognize them either—she never chatted with them, or greeted them with any particular warmth. Along with their polite smiles, these women also left behind that intense smell, which lingered inside the elevator and along the hallway long after they'd gone. Several times, F saw strangers from the building holding their noses, questioning where the terrible stench had come from, and it was as if Grandma were leaning over all the way from where she lived, her lips brushing F's cheek, as she whispered like God into her ear: *You'd better not forget me.*

It had always puzzled F that her stay-at-home mother never once made the trip out of the city to see her own mother. A few times, F had suggested that maybe they ought to send

Grandma a gift of some sort, to show they were thinking of her even if they couldn't spare the time for a visit. Her mother never responded. Later in the evening, she would solemnly rise from her armchair and go to open a drawer at the bottom of the television unit, where she kept a little notebook filled with scribbled-down numbers. How much longer until the mortgage is paid off? she would inquire, while also warning F that, if she had any broken furniture or electrical items, she'd better get them fixed or replace them.

F had a dim memory of Grandma as the complete opposite of her serious, untalkative mother. Grandma had a cheery voice and an easy, bubbly laugh, and loved to strike up conversations with strangers. She walked immense distances at great speed. But F couldn't remember what she looked like. Whenever she tried, all she could picture were bubbles fizzing inside a glass bottle. What were those dark, juice-like liquids contained within the glass? Sometimes they would be dark red, other times more of a yellowy orange. The smell altered too, but there were always those tiny orbs inside.

Any time F crouched down to examine the drink more carefully and was hit once again by the pungent, sour smell, she had a vague recollection of seeing exactly the same kind of bottle as a child. There had been hundreds of them, big and small, stacked up on top of one another in a very warm room.

Grown-up women were huddled together inside, drinking from the bottles. They wore loose linen clothes that let their thighs and breasts slip casually into view, filling the room with a strong, meaty scent. F had not connected the sour smell with the tea, instead assuming that it came from the women's bodies. She would bring her nose even closer to the bottle. She liked the smell and the warm childhood memory it evoked but, at the same time, had to admit there was something nauseating about it.

While F was growing up, Grandma's special deliveries had arrived exclusively for her mother. F did not dare touch them. Instead, she became very familiar with her mother's methods: pour refrigerated tea into a small cup, then drink in tiny sips. The tiny sips were not to savor the taste, but to avoid overdoing things. On her first try, F had knocked it back like water, and the moment it hit the back of her throat she knew it had been a mistake. Almost instantly, her head felt swollen and chills went through her stomach. She forced herself to stay calm, feeling the gaze of her mother from the opposite corner of the living room, scrutinizing her reactions. Her mother was waiting for her to mess up, just like when she used to watch her doing homework or practicing the piano.

Of course, what F was feeling wasn't really swelling or chills. Her body was going through the subtle internal transformations familiar only to someone who's tried the drink before. She closed her eyes, leaned her head as far back as possible, spread her arms along the back of her chair, and managed not to make a sound.

When she opened her eyes again, her mother had left the living room. The empty imprint of her body sat mutely on the leather sofa, and leafy strands of potted fern dangled silently from the top of the built-in cupboard. F and her mother's coexistence seemed perpetually shrouded in a fine, silk-screened silence. F often had the feeling that she was surrounded by clues—the shadows inside the apartment, or the way her book pages shuddered in a breeze. They were clues like the ones her mother gave when she scowled, or barked one of her short, cold laughs, to indicate that F had fallen short of her expectations. But clues being clues, she could never fully grasp what they meant.

Many people find school nightmarish, especially convent school, but F had loved it. She loved how the rules were so clearly laid out, numbered from one to one hundred. Even as a very young child, all she had needed was for the rules to be clearly laid out. Once she knew which direction she should be crawling in, she would crawl there the fastest. F loved competitions, loved rankings, was always determined to be the best. But as she advanced through school, she came to realize that school competitions were not real life. Real-life competitions didn't have clearly defined rules, or if they did they were unspoken ones, and any black-and-white guidelines were merely there to obfuscate the truth. Wasn't that right? One day everyone was still wiping their noses on the backs of their hands, and the next all the girls had turned bashful and cautious. They were like pretty gift boxes, with their real selves folded up neatly, secretly inside. Even the girl F had considered the most ordinary of them all suddenly exuded a powerful allure, seeming to broadcast the message that she was in possession of something, and if you wanted it, you would have to pay the price.

Where had the girls learned their tricks? Maybe, while F was diligently taking notes in class and they appeared to be slumped over their desks napping, they were actually in secret training, acquiring skills F had no idea about, being selected for competitions she was barred from entering. Were boys the prizes in these competitions? That didn't always seem to be the case. F had noticed that even though the girls would hold hands with boys, their eyes would wander; their gazes would settle somewhere else.

When she first started working, F would occasionally attend parties hosted by her former classmates. She was always so tired that she had to drag herself along, hair a tangled mess, eyes threaded with blood vessels. The other girls were all fluttering eyelashes, gentle wafts of perfume, fastidiously made-up faces. They no longer joked about F ending up a lonely old spinster; it was less funny now that it seemed like it might come true. Anyway, their elegant postures and the jewels flashing at their wrists and necks made the point for them. Talking had become a kind of taboo. Instead they would glance at one another, or touch elbows, in echoes of their mischievous schoolgirl selves. Eventually, keeping her tone deliberately lighthearted, one might ask F, "Haven't found anyone to your liking yet?"

The real meaning being: Had she had sex yet? F kept her eyes on the rainbow hues of their fingernails and tried to maintain a neutral expression behind her glasses.

Some secrets were not for sharing. For example, after F tried the sour tea for the first time, she knew it was an activity best kept to herself. For courtesy's sake, she wouldn't even drink it in front of her mother.

Every so often, she would bring her thermos with her to the park, or to the roof of her office building, but mostly she drank alone in her bedroom. That way, she could lie back on her bed afterward, enjoying the sensation of her body slipping into its altered state. Sometimes she felt like the tea had turned her into a different lifeform, without any bones, a soft sea creature with slippery, permanently moist skin. Sometimes she felt transformed into the ocean itself, like she was a flowing liquid without any defined shape. Sometimes she felt like an oil slick, like all she needed was a tiny spark and she'd roar into flames.

She would take the glass bottle from the fridge and pour the tea into a tumbler, stopping when she had about as much as a shot of whiskey. Then she would go into her room and place the glass on her bedside cabinet, lean back against her headboard, and spread her legs, imitating the kind of wanton pose she'd seen in porn films. She greeted the drink with tiny sips. It was a rare luxury. She had to be restrained about it because her mother was always sneaking around to check on the bottles, monitoring the liquid levels inside them. F was aware of her mother's activities because she did the same thing herself: if she looked in the fridge and saw there was slightly less tea than before, she knew that her mother had been chasing her own secret pleasure. Her mother experienced the same cravings as she did. The thought was both soothing and utterly terrifying.

But the woman on the platform didn't seem concerned at all. After downing a few mouthfuls, she passed the thermos to the little girl on the floor, as though offering her a toy.

F grabbed her hand.

"Are you sure about giving her this kind of tea?"

"Tea?" The woman laughed but made no further comment, as though they'd reached an understanding.

"So you've tried this...stuff before, have you?" asked F.

"Of course! Everyone in our town knows about her and her special tea."

The woman spoke in F's mother's dialect. F still couldn't see her face, but she felt an intimacy spring up between them. As the woman talked on about *her* and the goings-on in the little town where she lived, F realized that the *her* couldn't be anyone other than Grandma.

"I haven't seen her in such a long time," she lamented.

The woman suggested that F come with her to pay a visit.

"Her town's not far from here. And if you catch the early train out tomorrow morning, you'll still make it to wherever it is you're headed."

F shook her head. "Thank you for the thought, but..."

"It's already so late!" insisted the woman. "Don't tell me you have to work tonight?"

F hesitated. Her first meeting was fixed for the following afternoon; her only real reason for arriving a day early had been to spend an evening relaxing in the hotel, in preparation for the day to come. In which case, if she really wanted to see Grandma, wouldn't this be the perfect opportunity?

"And would you look at that, the train—"

A knife-like screech inserted itself into the conversation, brutally severing the end of the woman's sentence. Well, no, maybe the train wasn't as hard and sharp as all that; it was more like a snake, darting out of a dream into the cave of the waking world. Its head was so enormous and all-encompassing that F felt a sudden desire for it to stick out its tongue and wrap her up in it, then pull her down into its belly. She had not known she harbored a desire to be prey before. It didn't feel like she was picking up her bag and climbing onto the train; it felt like she was willingly, delightedly allowing the train to swallow her whole.

Once inside, F could tell immediately that this train was nothing like the one she'd been on earlier. Was there something wrong with the air-conditioning? The train car was warm and cozy, and so old that its walls were coated in a comforting layer of grease. There were no harsh fluorescent lights or passengers caressing the screens of electronic devices. Instead, the dim overhead lighting seemed designed specifically to lull people to sleep. The seats looked especially soft and comfortable. The few passengers on board were all fast asleep, arms and legs lolling into the aisles. After so long without a good night's rest, F had the feeling she'd entered a special sleeping room, laid out just for her. Why would she be worried about work? What did she care about muscle training and the ugly, ridiculous Power Rod anyway?

She followed the woman and little girl into a compartment, where the seats were incredibly wide and smelled like new leather. Stroking the fabric was like stroking an affectionate little pet.

"I must get some sleep," she murmured, very softly, only to herself, and yet somehow the woman heard her.

"Rest now," said the woman, as though soothing a child. "I'll wake you up before we arrive."

F felt a hand reach out to close her eyes, and her breathing began to deepen. Then her eyes snapped open.

"But it's all been such a rush," she said anxiously. "I don't have a gift for Grandma."

In the low lighting, she could see the woman and the little girl sitting opposite, hand in hand, smiling identical smiles. F was very, very sleepy; half her body was already gone, already dreaming. Who was it that took her hand? As she drifted off, she thought she heard the woman whisper, ever so faintly, with her brilliant red lips: "...but you're the greatest gift of all."

*

F watched line after line of leafless trees racing past the train windows, a few insolent branches scraping lightly against the glass. They were like ink erasers, rubbing against her already translucent memories until they were completely gone. What lay ahead? The aim of this unintended journey was no longer clear. All F had was the crumpled sheet of paper, spread out in front of her, and on that piece of paper, an illegible name.

She glanced at the man opposite, who was as lifeless as an empty sack. At some point, his head had drooped forward. Now his face was angled toward his open palm, as though it were a book he was reading. Clearly, he had invested all his energy into interpreting the stories those palm lines were telling in his dreams.

I can't be like him, she thought. I mustn't fall asleep again. Before this train goes much farther, I've got to get off and figure out where I'm going.

She decided to get off at the next stop.

The train slammed on its brakes. Soundlessly, the doors at the front of the train car sprung open, like a voiceless throat trying desperately to scream. Most passengers didn't even stir. Aside from F, no one stood up. She marched toward the exit with her bag.

Once the train had gone, vanishing into the distance like a hazy memory, all that remained on the platform were hundreds of intersecting shadows, dancing with every gust of wind. Looking up, F saw trees towering over them, still covered in leaves. Apparently the bleakness of autumn had not yet extended this far. The tracks in front of her were like a sturdy belt, linking two different worlds: in the direction the train had come from, there was a gloomy, seemingly never-ending forest; in the other, scattered houses and spots of light.

If the woman had left the train at Grandma's stop, then surely all F needed to do was follow the tracks backward and eventually she'd end up in Grandma's town. But she had stopped caring very much about finding Grandma. She decided to walk toward the houses. The sky was full of red clouds and she knew it wouldn't be long until dark. For now, the most important thing was to find somewhere to stay, preferably a guesthouse of some kind, somewhere she could rest before continuing her journey in the morning. With this plan in mind, she felt calmer, and even began to enjoy the changing colors of the sunset.

The path was easy enough to find, and before long F was outside a cake shop. Its doors were open and several baking trays filled with neat rows of pastries were on display outside, each pastry stamped with a little red flower. The whole place was in complete silence. F realized that, aside from some instant noodles on the first train, she hadn't eaten a thing since leaving the house early that morning. At the sight of the pretty red pastries, she felt a stab of hunger. She called into the shop a few times, but no one answered. She looked up and down the street, hoping to catch someone as they passed by, but all she saw was a portable clothes rack full of women's clothing. A plastic soccer ball lay in the middle of the road, half-eaten by a drain. F picked up a pastry and took a little bite.

"Delicious," she murmured, as if informing the shop. But she couldn't tell what the filling was. She took another bite. Even after eating two whole pastries, she still had no idea about the filling. She wasn't as hungry anymore but took another two, dropping them into a paper bag that she found inside. If she did happen to find Grandma, at least she'd have something to give her.

At this point, she noticed she was standing on something painted on the ground. A red arrow. There was another one, not much farther ahead. Maybe they were children's doodles, or some kind of sign used in the village, but she followed them as if they had been drawn specifically for her. The wind was strong and she had to struggle to walk against it. She hadn't made it very far when her stomach began to growl, and before she knew it, she had eaten both of Grandma's pastries.

Eventually, the arrows led her to a wall. The sky was dark now and she couldn't determine the exact color of the wall, but she could see a dark crack running across it, like a seam. When she reached out to touch it, she heard a voice inside call out: "Come in!"

It was definitely a woman's voice, although it was hard to guess her age. What had seemed to be a crack turned out to be the edge of the doorframe. F hesitated. There was a strong, unsettling smell that made her want to turn and run. But if she abandoned this place, who knew whether she'd find anywhere else to spend the night?

F had not yet made up her mind when the door swung open. The woman who had opened it immediately turned and started walking away before F could get a look at her face. It was too dark to see much of anything, anyway. F could vaguely make out a garden, a few low buildings and, in between the buildings, shifting human outlines. The woman didn't say anything, just kept walking. F followed. They arrived at one of the buildings.

The woman opened a door on the ground floor. F had assumed it would lead to an entrance hall but instead it led directly to a room. The room had no windows and was almost impossibly tiny, even tinier than a room you might find in the city. The door was tiny too, and F had to duck slightly as she entered. Once inside, however, it felt different, not quite so small, wrapping snugly around her body like a tight-fitting dress. It felt good. But she quickly became aware that the coziness was not only due to the size; it was also the temperature. She stroked one of the walls. They couldn't be concrete; it had to be another, softer material, because there was no hint of cold beneath her palm. It was as though there were another hand inside the wall, reaching out to grip hers.

The room contained only a single bed and a small desk with a lamp. There were no pillows or bedclothes on the bed.

"We don't use pillows here, and it gets so hot in the evening that you won't be needing sheets either. In fact, many guests end up stripping all their clothes off in the middle of the night."

The woman had stayed outside the door, out of sight. F thought her remarks seemed unlikely, given that it was late autumn. Then again, it really was warm in there. F wished she could take off her jacket. As soon as the woman had left, she made sure the door was closed, then quickly removed both her jacket and her trousers. She sat down on the bed in just her blouse, feeling much more relaxed.

She knew she ought to rest, but she had that meeting the next day. She opened her bag and took out a file, intending to skim through it by the light of the desk lamp. But maybe the light was too dim—the characters melded into spots and shadows, writhing like a cluster of insects about to fly off the page.

F put down the file, feeling exhausted. Or at least like she had no energy to concentrate. Despite appearances, the bed was exceptionally comfortable. She took off her glasses and leaned back. Exceptionally soft and springy. Almost flesh-like. And—but was this another trick of the light?—the color of the bed seemed almost a perfect match for her skin. She sank into the mattress, and it was as though the room had opened a large toothless mouth and swallowed her up.

Just as she was about to fall asleep, her eyes cracked open. The door didn't seem to be closed properly. She went over and discovered that the frame seemed to have warped with age, so that the door no longer fit perfectly into it. No matter how hard she tried to make the door stay closed, it would slowly work its way out again. It was as if there were someone behind it, stealthily pulling it open.

F went back to bed. It didn't matter. She was so tired that a pack of wolves could be waiting for her outside the door and she'd still want to get some sleep first. Then, maybe because of the heat, or else the long-distance travel, her crotch started to itch, compelling her to squeeze her thighs together and rub them back and forth. Her breathing grew labored, she couldn't suppress her moans, and the whole room seemed to squirm in sync with her rhythm. It was getting so hot. It was so hot that F could no longer stand it and went over to kick the door wide open.

A refreshing, cold wind blew in from outside, although it carried with it that strong, unsettling smell. Without putting her clothes back on, F walked out of the room, feeling the icy dew attack her legs. It was pitch black, but after a few minutes her eyes began to adjust, and she could recognize shapes lurking in the darkness. A paved path: a few perfectly round rocks glimmering with a greenish light. She followed the path. The smell grew even stronger.

She reached a warehouse with a roof that sloped down on either side. She watched a woman stride out through the wide-open door, carrying something. Then another woman walked in. F followed. There were a lot of women walking around inside the warehouse, as well as a few sitting on the floor or on top of packing cases, laughing and chatting among themselves. All over the floor and all over the shelves were glass bottles, countless glass bottles, each one covered with a piece of gauze kept in place by an elastic band.

"Has something gone bad in here?" asked F, covering her nose with her hand.

"On the contrary," said one of the women, turning to face her, "they're all still growing."

That was when F realized that she didn't need to cover her nose; she didn't hate the smell, after all. She inhaled deeply. She should have recognized it before: it was the smell of Grandma's sour tea, just even more intense.

A woman stood in front of a short-necked, unsealed bottle,

holding a plate in one hand and a pair of tongs in the other. She was using the tongs to pick up something from the plate. It was about the diameter of a rice bowl, perfectly circular, moist, smooth, flesh-like. The woman waved it about, as if to make sure that F had noticed it. F tried to look more closely—no, it wasn't just like flesh, it was like flesh with the skin peeled off: a clitoris-pink, newborn thing. She watched as the woman dropped it into the bottle.

"It's the mother. It'll slowly reproduce and grow inside the bottle. That's why we cover the bottles with gauze instead of sealing them with lids—we have to let it breathe. The mother sucks in nutrients from the tea and then gives birth to more flesh. It's the offspring of flesh and water."

F looked inside the bottle. The mother had been poked into the liquid by the woman's long tongs, but it gradually rose to the surface. Bubbles trembled beneath it. It felt oddly familiar, like something F had seen a long time before.

"Who buys all this tea?" she asked.

The woman with the tongs laughed, and her laughter seemed to infect the other women, traveling around them like a wave.

"This isn't even enough for us! What would we be selling it for?" said the woman. "Little girl, it's time for you to go back to bed. If you stay around here much longer, I can't guarantee we won't slice off your flesh to make a mother."

F couldn't suppress a smile. She was over forty; who did they think they were calling *little girl*? But then, somehow, her body did feel much lighter and smaller than before. She thought of a game she used to play with Grandma when she was little. Grandma would take out a knife and pretend to slice off her arm.

"Come on," Grandma would say, "this bit's for me!"

Had the mothers all been sliced off the women's bodies?

A woman ladled out a little cup of liquid from one of the bottles and pressed it into F's hands with a wink. F could feel its warmth through the cup. It bubbled fiercely. She carried it out of the warehouse into the night. There were no longer any stones outside to guide her, but even so, she quickly arrived back in her room.

She climbed into bed and took a little sip, then put the cup down on her bedside cabinet and took off all her clothes. The room wasn't just hot, it was humid. In fact, the bed felt almost waterlogged. And the moisture was coming from her body; it wasn't sweat, it was meat stock, flowing from her pores. The sour smell in the room had become so overpowering that F imagined herself in the belly of the building, slowing dissolving into its stomach juices. By morning, her whole body would be gone; it would have become part of the room.

The door slowly cracked open, like the slit of a half-opened eye. Maybe one of the women was behind it, spying on her. But there was no face, only a voice, which seemed to come to her from very far away, sneaking close, all the way into her ears. Was it Grandma? What a pity she had eaten those pastries. What would she give her now?

"...you're the greatest gift of all," whispered the God-like voice.

F closed her eyes. It was a dark-red liquid and the bubbles kept on rising. F saw her own body: it had no teeth anymore, no bones, it was just flesh, and all that was left was a tiny piece, so soft, and because her lips were all gone now, she couldn't even describe how incomparably wonderful it felt.

Auntie Han's Modern Life

嫻姨的現代生活

Enoch Tam

Translated by Jeremy Tiang

就在太陽完全沒入山後，大馬路只留下一線又一線的浮影，而E區，也隨著太陽的消隱，剩下黑黑的一個洞。

"When the sun was completely gone and the road was reduced to a series of dim lines, there was nothing left of District E but a cavernous hole."

Back when Auntie Han was still Miss Han, she already had a shop in District E. At the time, District E was firmly within City H, and the thrumming of needle and thread filled the neighborhood day and night.

One time, Miss Han left her shop not long before sunrise. People say the darkness before the dawn is darker than anything else on earth, and she knew this to be true because the food stalls of District E always turned their lamps up to their brightest at this hour. Kin was waiting for her at the breakfast place. He usually worked through the night, then came here for a meal that could be breakfast, lunch, dinner, or supper.

Miss Han and Kin didn't get to see much of each other. Every day, Kin had to ship crates of clothing from the northern mainland to City H. With practiced technique, he would zoom in and out of the various districts, before finally turning onto the road that led to E. As he drove along, his cab speakers blared stirring theme songs from kung fu movies. After about fifteen tracks, he'd arrive at District E, where figures loomed out of the darkness to take the goods from him. These people were tattooed with dragons or phoenixes and often had cigarettes dangling from their lips, especially in the winter. On windy nights, breathing in hot smoke warmed your innards, easing the work a little. Kin only ever got to District E when the streetlights were blazing, so he'd never seen its bustling roads when the shops were full of customers.

As for Miss Han, she never saw the people unloading goods in the night. All she knew was, when she returned to her shop each morning, her stock was waiting outside in neatly stacked crates. She just had to roll up the shutters, and business could resume. She did the briskest trade around lunchtime, when all the shops in the row were open, and the street was throbbing with people, people, and still more people. Even more people kept pouring in. Once, Miss Han had to get some stock from the upper balcony, and when she looked down, she thought there could be no sight more beautiful than the surging crowds beneath her. Even after she became Auntie Han, she never again saw anything so stunning.

Inevitably, the street emptied out before sunset, and the shops would shut one by one, owners and assistants heading home. The spaces that had contained crates of clothes transformed as darkness fell, acquiring lights, counters, stools, and stoves. Then the cooking began. After the supper rush, it was the turn of truckload after truckload of goods to arrive. Parking, unloading, stacking. The trucks pulled away just as the sun peeked over the hilltops, and the neighborhood moved from dark to light once more.

After unloading his truck that day, Kin parked outside Miss Han's shop, then sat at a nearby food stall to wait for her. He thought he could sense her nearby, feeding strip after strip of cloth through her sewing machine, allowing the needle to jab in and out, then scissoring a shape and sending it through the machine once more. Kin sat there and thought he could hear the needle piercing the fabric. As he sat waiting for Miss Han to finish her work, he couldn't quite resist his drowsiness and kept nodding off.

Over the last few years, Miss Han had managed to acquire the shop, finally becoming the boss herself. Now she was the one ordering other people to move the stock around, to buy and sell. On this day, an international customer had shown up, and she'd had to jump off her stool and hurry over, using her limited English to find out what he wanted. After much noisy jabbering and pantomiming, Miss Han understood that this foreigner was planning to order some stock he could sell in his own country, and he was hoping she could run up some samples. And so, after her employees left that night, Miss Han had to stay back all on her own, cutting and sewing, trying her best to get the samples done in time to show the visitor the next day.

Finally, Kin heard the needle stop, then Miss Han walked through the door and came over to sit across from him. She ordered noodles with fried egg and spam and yawned widely. By the time the food arrived, she'd yawned seventeen more times. Kin was animatedly describing his encounter with a warehouse manager, how he'd said such-and-such to persuade him to place an order, then such-and-such to get him to lower the price. Just as he got to the most exciting part, Miss Han finished her noodles and returned to her shop, where she would try to nap for an hour or two.

As the sun poked its head above the hills of District E, and the land turned from dark to light once more, Miss Han woke up and opened her shop. Now she would wait for the foreign customer to show up again, along with the good luck he would bring her.

At some point later on, without her noticing when exactly, people stopped calling her Miss Han and started addressing her, familiarly, as Auntie Han. And, also without her knowing exactly how it happened, her shop became a bazaar for secondhand goods. What she did remember, though, was the night her shop transformed, District E suddenly vanished. That day, when the laden trucks turned onto the road leading in, they saw nothing before them, just a darkness their headlights couldn't illuminate. The food-stall owners raised their lanterns high and turned them up as bright as they would go but still couldn't see their usual spots. After this, the trucks stopped coming, and the stall owners set up business elsewhere. As for Auntie Han, when she heard all the rumors the next day about District E closing down, she went back to her shop as usual, and there was District E, as if it had never vanished. Everyone knew, though, that when the sun sank beneath the hills again, when the faint moonbeams were blotted out, District E would disappear once more.

Like the other truck drivers, Kin stopped coming to District E.

Now it was buses that rumbled down the road to District E, and only a few people ever alighted. Some would hesitate for a moment in front of Auntie Han's shop, but most just hurried off to work. The crowds of bygone days were no more, replaced by rush-hour commuters who now and then lingered at the outlet shops. This was the brief portion of the day when Auntie Han would swiftly raise the sign that had never once changed, "Going Out of Business Sale, Final Day," hoping to lure the office ladies into thinking this opportunity would never come again, so they would buy a few more items.

After the commuters dispersed, the shutters of District E would rattle down one after another. Auntie Han and her neighbors would return to their box homes in the hills, leaving a row of metal shutters to await darkness and disappearance.

The villagers liked living in those squat square boxes, evenly spaced and slowly moving. Yes, over the years, the houses had crept along the hills all by themselves, as if to protect the ancient grave behind them. None of the villagers had ever seen this grave, but it existed in the legends that passed between them. As for whether it contained treasure or a lost history, no one had any idea. Quite a few people had tried venturing into the hills in search of this tomb, and some government officials had investigated too, but the houses always seemed to know when someone was embarking on a hunt and would shift around ahead of time to block the paths. Trails that used to lead up into the hills would twist around and end up back on the main road.

Auntie Han had never thought about seeking out the ancient tomb, but whenever the houses shifted into a new configuration, she would follow along and have a look. She liked exploring the alleyways that looked both familiar and new to her. Even though the houses were old and their exterior walls had peeled badly over the decades, she'd never considered leaving. Every time she came home, she felt as if it were to a different house on a different street.

Later on, the garden-keepers planted a couple of skyscrapers in front of the village, blocking the path of the restless houses.

Auntie Han knew the houses had been in low spirits for a while. Some were even depressed enough that they stopped moving altogether. The others did everything they could to remind their moribund companions of all the times they'd worked together to thwart the humans and how satisfying it had felt to be constantly mobile. But the sad, silent houses remained sad and silent, which made the active ones feel as if a bucket of water had been flung over them, and gradually they grew inactive too.

Some time later, the garden-keepers sent subordinates who went around measuring everything, though it was unclear whether they were calculating how much space the houses occupied or trying to work out where this ancient grave was.

Kin came back to District E alongside the garden-keepers' minions.

Auntie Han was startled to see him again. How had he managed to conceal the dragons and phoenixes that covered his body beneath a white shirt and dark suit? It was only later that she found out: the disappearance of District E had been a wake-up call for Kin. All of a sudden, he'd realized he couldn't spend the rest of his life as a long-haul trucker, so he threw in his lot with the garden-keepers. Back then, they were just a small outfit that went around planting flowers and hadn't yet reached the point of cultivating entire skyscrapers.

That day, Auntie Han ended up sitting with Kin at a roadside stall as he looked all around, waxing nostalgic.

"So it looks like the hills around District E haven't changed."

"Right, they haven't changed."

"The noodles with fried egg and spam haven't changed either."

"Yes, a bowl of noodles is still a bowl of noodles."

"Those houses of yours don't seem to be moving around anymore."

"True, the houses no longer move."

"And your shop? Are you still doing business with those foreigners?"

Actually, Auntie Han had never done business with any foreigners. That one visitor from abroad had never returned, so she knew good luck wouldn't arrive for her in this lifetime. That was fine, she didn't need good luck. As long as she could put up her "Going Out of Business Sale, Final Day" sign every day, she would be all right. Her life was more than halfway over. If she could hold on to her shop and go on living in the hills of District E, then her days would pass as they always had.

And what's more, Auntie Han knew that the garden-keepers hadn't sent their lackeys to survey the villagers' property or to seek out the ancient tomb. They were here to find the legendary water source that lay beneath the grave. The garden-keepers had bought up the land around District E long ago, every scrap of it including the plot her shop was on. By his third glass of beer, Kin was babbling to her, flushed and exhilarated, that the reason the garden-keepers hadn't confiscated her land yet was because they still hadn't uncovered the water source.

"Those stories have been around for a long time. Everyone who says they're in E to find the tomb, government or not, is actually looking for groundwater. The garden-keepers knew I was born here, so they asked me to snoop around. All those years going in and out of E, though, I hadn't heard anything about it. But the garden-keepers told me there was enough water under the surface that, if they could tap into it, all the soil around here would become super fertile, and then they'd be able to plant skyscrapers even taller and more magnificent than those ones over there. When that happens, they'll take all this land back and grow buildings on it. You'll probably get a unit or two for yourself if that happens! Better than your little secondhand shop, anyway."

Before he could descend any further into nonsense, Kin passed out with a clunk on the counter. The sun dropped in the west, the row of shops lowered their shutters, and everyone hurried out into the street. Auntie Han continued sitting where she was, watching the dark of night languidly devouring the road. When the sun was completely gone and the road was reduced to a series of dim lines, there was nothing left of District E but a cavernous hole.

Auntie Han spent the entire drunken night with Kin, waiting for the sun to appear above the hills in the other direction. When it finally showed up, the green hills were suddenly bleached pale, and Auntie Han imagined she saw white elephants parading along the slopes, slowly melting into little hillocks. Kin, now utterly plastered, pointed at the sun and slurred, I've found the water, I've found the water! Auntie Han smiled quietly as she hefted Kin back to her house. Along the way, she thought she saw the elephants on the opposite hills waving their trunks, as if they were saying goodbye, or perhaps beckoning her toward them.

Lip Service

吐字表演

Zhu Hui
Translated by Michael Day

含逸若不胜风，几乎语不成句，所有的标点符号被打落一床。

"Hanyi's words wouldn't form sentences, as if the wind had blown them to bits, scattering the sheets with punctuation marks."

THEY SAY FLATTERY IS A SKILL EVERY MAN SHOULD HAVE, but truly beautiful women are rare, so words of praise don't always come easily. That's why this advice was written: if she isn't pretty, praise her figure; if her figure is no good, say she's sweet; if there's nothing good about her at all, just say she's smart, with a pure heart and a nice personality. You might call this advice cynical, but you have to admit it's clever. With Hanyi, though, none of this was needed, because she was a true beauty, a genuinely gorgeous woman with a stunning face, a graceful figure, and a great personality. The Chinese language has no shortage of colorful phrases for female beauty: beauty that brings down states and ruins cities, a heavenly fragrance suffusing the land, a light to outshine the moon, grace to shame a swan. But these are exaggerations. Simply put, when you saw Hanyi your eyes would light up, not just because she was stunning but because she was on TV, and the screen was so bright.

Hanyi was a news anchor. A TV news anchor for the provincial station. The leading lady. She had been working the job for twelve years. In twelve years, TVs had changed generations again and again, from CRT to plasma to LCD, but Hanyi had not changed—you could toss out your old TV, but when you brought home the new one and turned it on, there she was, the same as always. Unless you didn't watch the news at all, you'd see her there nearly every day at the same time, in the same place, wherever in your home you kept your TV. Many men went ages without glancing at their wives, but each day they all took a good look at Hanyi.

Hanyi's channel had long since been picked up by satellite, so you could watch it anywhere in China. Maybe not everyone in the country knew her. Maybe there were even some in the province who didn't, but there at least, she was a household name. *Daily Highlights* was on at 6:30 every evening, and *On Air* was on at noon, so on a regular day you'd have no fewer than two dates with Hanyi. Riding invisible airwaves, she would arrive in your home at exactly the appointed time, maybe the living room, maybe the bedroom. Her measured newscaster's diction would fill your home with pleasing, practiced tones. Everyone was used to her voice, and if one day a different voice delivered the international, national, or provincial news, it just didn't sound right, and you wouldn't quite trust it. Her voice had a certain authority. Speaking of Hanyi's voice, it had a rare charm. What was charming about it was not just its pleasing sound, but its versatility. As a TV newscaster, it went without saying that she spoke in a rich, clear, serious tone, but what set her voice apart was that it could also turn warm and familiar, and in the second half of the program, which often told stories of ordinary people's lives, Hanyi's voice would naturally take on that familiar tone, with a lilting cadence, a nurturing quality, a "girl next door" kind of voice.

It was startling that these two voices came from the same person. They say opera singers can't sing pop, and it's about as easy for a donkey to dance as it is for a pop star to sing opera. But Hanyi smoothly adjusted her cadence, masterfully adapting to different types of news. In general, her voice was polished, sweet, and smooth, but if you listened closely, at times you could hear the elegance of classical poetry, like a row of white egrets in the blue sky, or two golden orioles singing in the willows; at other times it had the driving quality of a revolutionary march, while at still others it turned mellow and warm. For many people, this warmth was like being surrounded by the sweet song of an oriole, like bathing in the bright winter sun.

Somehow, she'd held on to her seat at the anchor's desk for twelve years. Twelve years later, she was still sitting bolt upright, staring straight at the camera. When TV viewers looked at Hanyi, they saw her sitting with carefree poise, but inside she wasn't quite so carefree. She saw young girls sprouting up one after the next, each more beautiful and capable than the one before, each covetously eyeing her seat at the news desk. In twelve years, Hanyi had been through four different male co-anchors, and in fact her voice had changed too. People who liked her said it had an even more powerful magnetism, especially at the tail ends of sentences, where it had gotten a little husky, a little rough. Put bluntly, it was showing signs of age. She couldn't control this roughness, but she could control how she looked and acted at the news desk. She spent longer and longer at the mirror, slathering on makeup. Her tone turned more solemn for the serious stories and warmer for the lighthearted parts, as if to grab the viewers and pull them close. She used a solemn tone not just because the story demanded it, but because of her own needs. There was self-righteousness in her tone, as if she were convinced the seat at the anchor's desk was rightfully hers. Recently, she'd made slight adjustments to her delivery of political stories, infusing her solemn tone with an intimate feel, even to the point of casual indifference, so that you would have sworn she was personally acquainted with the well-known figures she named in her stories. She hinted at high-level connections, hoping this would check the scheming of her would-be usurpers, but Hanyi herself knew well that though she and the station director were close, she had no friends in higher places. Inevitably a sense of unease seeped into her delivery. She couldn't control it. At the end of the broadcast, she would say goodbye to the audience, tilting her head slightly, drawing in her chin, and nodding deeply. "Ladies and gentlemen, this has been *On Air*, and I'm Hanyi. Goodbye!" The nod in particular came across as so gentle, so sincere, that she even seemed to be begging for approval.

The opening credits of *On Air* showed a bird's-eye view of the province wreathed in swirling clouds, suggesting the heavens of the Taoist immortals, but Hanyi did not live in the clouds. When the broadcast ended, she took off the headset, left the studio, and went home. She walked not on clouds but city streets filled with mud, garbage, and potholes. Although Sifangcheng, where she lived, was an upmarket area, water pooled in the streets when it rained, and if she wasn't careful a passing car would spatter her skirt with filthy water.

For the past few days it had been raining constantly. It was the rainy season, so that was not unusual. If it was nothing but a light, steady patter, water wouldn't pool in the road, but even a slightly heavy morning rain would back up the drainage system. At the time she had been thinking only of the neighborhood's high social status, and it hadn't occurred to her that its low geography could be a problem. On top of that the workers had cut corners, and the building seemed due to start falling apart any day. At least Hanyi's home on the twentieth floor was close enough to the heavens that the rising waters posed no threat.

She was still in a breezy mood when she left home that morning. Her husband was the president of an electric company, and he started work early. She'd usually lie around until ten or so before leaving for work. *On Air* started at noon, and she only had to be there an hour ahead of time. She ate breakfast, cleaned herself up a bit, and headed for the door, grabbing her sunglasses. Since she'd gotten famous, she never neglected to wear her sunglasses when she went out. The glasses were big, covering nearly a third of her face, showing the world she was famous, and saving her eyes the work of smiling when she saw someone she knew. After locking the door, but before putting on her glasses, she saw two people standing in the hall. At the moment they were peering out the window. Hanyi started, noticing the long suitcase at their feet. It was a little longer than a violin case. She stopped in her tracks, sensing something out of place. The man spoke sharply: "None of your business. Move along." Hanyi was hesitating over whether to go back inside and shut the door, or just keep walking, when the man who had spoken approached.

Hanyi's heart raced. She forced herself to stand her ground. Wearing a stern look, the man came to a stop right in front of her. "We're on government business." Then his eyes widened, and his face showed a hint of smile. "Oh, it's you?" Flustered, Hanyi nodded. She realized she'd been recognized. A bit calmer now, she said, "Sorry to trouble you." He smiled. "We'll let you get on your way." Hanyi hesitated a moment, then turned to leave. Casting a passing glance out the window, she scurried off.

She was no stranger to high-pressure situations. After all, she was famous, but in the end she was a woman, and maybe that's why she cracked under such insignificant pressure—so Hanyi told herself later. When she stepped into the elevator, she remembered that the man who had spoken to her had been holding a pair of binoculars, which was enough to show they weren't there for her sake. They were looking at something in the distance. They really were there on some kind of business. But what that business was, Hanyi had no idea.

Hanyi was in a worried mood that day. It wasn't that she was interested in government affairs. The public just happened to get the news of national and provincial politics from her because it was her job. She sat before the camera paying lip service to words someone else had written. She was a mouthpiece, a cog in the machine. She'd worked for a while on a news commentary show, but she'd panicked, thinking she'd been put out to pasture because of her age. She wanted to be back on the front lines, so she'd gone to the station director and made extraordinary appeals to quit. The station director had gone to the head of the news division and informed him that Hanyi wouldn't be working on current events shows anymore. Instead, she would fully dedicate herself to delivering the news. Her dedication meant stability. The stability of society could hang in the balance. The director had said emphatically, "Of course, your news department is important, but so is Hanyi's work. We're the ones who inform the common people about the policies of the national government and the actions of our leaders." He had flashed a good-humored grin. "You're important. We're all important. If a government leader does something and we don't report it, then in one sense they never did it. If a leader goes somewhere and we don't report it, as far as the people are concerned, they never went there." When all was said and done, he was a capable leader, and his talk had proved persuasive. For some reason, Hanyi suddenly recalled the station director's words—from the looks of it, what happened this morning meant some government fat cat was coming to the provincial capital. The two men with their equipment really were there on a special mission. It was none of Hanyi's business, of course, but she was curious: Who was it, bringing along such heavy security? She didn't want to guess what the VIP was there for, and she didn't have to. All she had to do was wait for the story to land on her desk.

In the blink of an eye she forgot all about that morning. Stability had been restored. She sat in the spacious office, chatting with coworkers and riffling through the paper. She received a draft of the news and finished the broadcast of *On Air*. She made no mistakes, and there was nothing special about the day's news. The only unpleasant thing was the call from her husband, asking if she'd seen the station director, if he had time to meet. She knew well what he wanted from the director. He worked in electrical engineering, and if you stripped away the concrete from the station building, what you'd see was a steel frame and a dense web of electric lines, her husband's bread and butter. In theory, Hanyi had no reason to oppose him, but she was annoyed by his persistence, and still more annoyed that he had to go through her. It was his needy tone, the way he made the responsibility hers. The station director was her boss, not the other way around. She sullenly refused his request to contact the director, threw down the phone, and went back to washing off her makeup. Her relationship with her husband was a little strange, neither hot nor cold. They never argued. He spent most of the workday out of the office, and she was sure he wasn't home at this hour. She was hesitating over whether to go home when her backup at the news desk, a girl the captions called Xiabo but everyone else called Bobo, walked up to her, nodded, and smiled. Then she sighed meaningfully. "Man, it's pouring buckets. This sucks! Time for a change!" As she spoke, she waved the staff duty chart in Hanyi's face, brushed past her, and walked off. Hanyi knew that she was scheduled to appear on today's *Daily Highlights*, and nothing on the chart was any of Bobo's business. She flashed a generous smile and walked away with her head held high.

But inside she was seething. On the way home, a passing car spattered mud on her skirt again. It was just her luck. She arrived home and prepared to go out shopping, hurriedly changing into a new set of clothes. She put on a new skirt with a matching top, shoes, and bag, and even a little makeup. This series of movements was dexterous and decisive, without a hint of hesitation, as if she'd gone home at midday just to change clothes, then go out on the town.

A fine drizzle had slickened the streets, which were crowded in spite of the wet weather. Many people went out just to go out, not because they wanted to go shopping, or because they needed something. Hanyi had heard men say so but hadn't believed it, thinking of it as typical male ignorance, or a man's excuse to keep his wallet shut. Often women went out without anything special in mind but came home with their arms full of shopping bags. Then they did have a purpose after all. And beautiful women like her gained more by going out than a bounty of shopping bags. They squirreled away the envious glances of passersby, especially the surprise and admiration in the eyes of men, and stored them in their hearts. They said little had changed since the days when men hunted and women gathered. Men had clear goals, and women just grabbed what they could. Face-to-face with a beautiful woman like Hanyi, in the broad light of day, men only dared pierce her with the arrows of their gaze. Each arrow of admiration added to Hanyi's store of confidence.

Hanyi radiated such poise and dignity that a spotlight seemed to follow her through the crowd. Her looks and attire exuded class, even the purse and sunglasses, marking her as well above white-collar. It wasn't just that she was rich. She had a certain elegance, an air of learning. It had been raining for days, and the crowded streets were like a giant hopscotch game, the pedestrians skipping and stepping around puddles. Hanyi smiled through pursed lips, her mood lightening a little. But suddenly, she hesitated. Where was she going, anyway? Her purse was stuffed full of cards, but she had no need to go shopping. The factory owners sent her an endless supply of free clothes. Some she wore just once on camera before hanging them in the closet. Should she go to the beauty salon? No, she wasn't in the mood. Beauty treatments were basically meant to deceive, and the price of their short-term effects was slathering your skin with chemicals and who knew what else, sure to cause no end of trouble in the future; if you were serious about it, you took a knife to your face, but Hanyi had no need for plastic surgery. She'd been born beautiful. Plastic surgery was a popular conversation topic among the women at the station. In general, those who talked about it hadn't done it, and those who did it didn't talk. But this rule had taken shape only gradually, and in the past there had been a few women who had egged each other on, steeling their courage and going to get surgery together. Back then Hanyi had just secured her seat at the news desk. She felt invincible. She'd yet to realize youth was slipping away. She liked to shoot the breeze as much as anyone, but she never took part in this talk—not only because she had no need for underhanded tricks, but because she took no pleasure in picking apart people's flaws. It felt to her like brazen derision. The more enthusiastically you took part, the more you seemed to be singing your own praises, looking down your nose at people. But on one occasion she couldn't help slipping in a comment, because her predecessor at the news desk kept steering the conversation back to her face. Hanyi couldn't stifle a laugh: "Hyaluronan, Botox, heheh." These words contained characters that, in other contexts, meant "piss" and "poison." She enunciated clearly and carefully: "Piss, poison—you're sick!" She pronounced the syllables with a distinct rhythm, giving each a measured weight. Xiabo had been truly just a girl then, hanging on Hanyi's every word. As the anchorwoman rolled her eyes in annoyance, Xiabo flattered her: "Hanyi has no need to slice and dice herself. Her mother's womb was the operating room. She made sure to do the job right before popping her out." Pretending to cradle Hanyi's face in her hands, she imitated the doting mother: "There there, little one, let's be modest, you're only the third most beautiful baby ever born." The whole room resounded with chortling, chuckling, every kind of laugh. These days, Xiabo's breasts seemed to be bulging bigger than ever, and by design or by chance, they were always swinging in Hanyi's face. Who knew if they were real?

There was a plastic surgeon's office just up the road. Hanyi gave it a passing glance. But in the span of this brief look, she made a discovery. From behind, she saw a familiar figure entering the clinic. Was it Xiabo? Hanyi wasn't sure. Xiabo had big boobs, but her nose was stubby, one of the many flaws in her appearance. Unlike a camel, her proud peaks weren't attached to her back, so there was no way to be certain it was her. Hanyi chuckled to herself, took a few steps forward, and stopped. She hoped secretly she and Xiabo might have a "chance meeting" on her way out. She recalled the joke that had made the rounds at the office a while back: "The elephant asked the camel, 'How come you have boobs growing from your back?' The camel replied, 'Screw you, at least I don't have a dick growing from my face!' Hearing this, the snake burst out laughing. Angrily, the elephant shot back, 'Look at you, you've got a face growing from your dick!'" Hanyi realized she'd draw attention if she kept hanging around, and she decided that since Xiabo didn't have boobs on her back, she wouldn't be a dick. Smiling to herself, she went on her way.

She still couldn't help laughing when she thought of the joke. The dirty-minded men at the station had had a ball with it, ribbing one another endlessly. Some men were like elephants, with dicks growing from their faces—their filthy thoughts were right on the surface. Others were like snakes, with faces covering their dicks—they wore stern, serious masks. In private, the station director was good-humored and easygoing. He had no taboos, and she recalled him relishing the joke. When she thought of this, Hanyi's face fell. A fine drizzle fell around her, and all at once the droplets felt heavy. It was a rain as fine as fog, but rather than calling up a romantic atmosphere, the weather instantly put her in a foul mood. Hanyi's unusual sexual relationship with the director was a secret at the station. Only a few other women knew about it. In private the director revealed himself as a man, one with a peculiar predilection. When her thoughts turned to his fetish, hackles rose from her skin. They spoke openly with one another, and no topic was off limits. Hanyi had joked with the director that according to the Chinese zodiac he must be a snake, because his face covered up his dick. The director had laughed loudly and said, well, I wish I were a snake, because that would make me a few years younger, and I wouldn't have to retire so soon. Then he had pronounced solemnly, "Snakes have nothing on me. You need to know something. Snakes have long dicks, but they're slippery and limp. Mine is nice and stiff. See for yourself!" When she recalled this, to her own surprise, her lips turned up in the hint of a smile. As she smiled, she cursed herself inside for being so cheap. She had no shame.

There are things you simply shouldn't think about. If you do, you can't keep on living, or at least, you can't keep on being a news anchor. Hanyi climbed the steps and went into the electronics store.

It was the slow season, and the store was nearly empty. The floor shone brilliantly in the entryway, reflecting the customers' wet footprints. Hanyi browsed around with no particular purpose. The compact appliances that were all the rage these days were displayed on the first floor because a pedestrian might happen by and decide to buy one; to purchase large appliances, you had to go upstairs. You had to know what you wanted, and go to the trouble of getting it. That's what life was like with the businessmen in charge. Hanyi smiled coldly to herself. You had to admit the businessmen knew what they were doing. As she stepped onto the escalator, she heard a familiar voice from far away.

It was a voice more familiar to her than any other—hers. TVs were stacked tier upon tier in a three-walled enclosure, each brighter and bigger than the next, the very biggest like a giant picture window, but instead of outdoor scenery, the view was of Hanyi, Hanyi's *On Air*. It was a repeat broadcast. That voice, that cadence, that pretty face, Hanyi knew them all so well, but at the moment that only made them stranger. Countless screens showed the same image, filling the three-walled enclosure with infinitely repeated images of her. They surrounded her, making the same gestures, speaking the same words. Hanyi hadn't come here today to see this spectacle, but she'd seen such things before in her twelve-year career, so she wasn't caught off guard. A few of the TVs, interspersed with the others for contrast, played high-definition landscape footage, making Hanyi part of the world's most beautiful scenery. She had to admit she liked the sight of it. For a moment she had a sense of unreality, as if she'd transformed into Sun Wukong, the monkey character from Journey to the West who created endless clones of himself by plucking his magic hairs. She smiled faintly and shook her head at the approaching salesman. She had the sudden urge to tell him, there's no need to turn on so many TVs, it's a waste. But she didn't. That was going too far, crossing the line into rudeness. She didn't even take her sunglasses off. She had long since lost the desire to be recognized. She didn't want to be talked to. If she had taken off the sunglasses, it would have been an invitation. She was getting ready to leave when the salesman approached again, carrying a pair of heavy glasses. It was a 3-D TV, he explained, it was just like real life, she had to see for herself. Hanyi waved him away, turned, and left. The real-life Hanyi had yet to reach the stairs when her cellphone rang. It was the director.

Hanyi knitted her brow, knowing the director couldn't see. His tone was the same as always. The Hanyi on TV kept talking with ease and confidence about "the national economy and the people's livelihood" and "the great enterprise of governance," and all of a sudden Hanyi had had it up to here. Phone pressed to her ear, she nearly ran down the stairs. The director had summoned her again, and though she tried to make excuses, she was left with no choice but to report for duty before leaving work that evening. In other words, after the broadcast of *Daily Highlights*, she would have to go in for "overtime." "Overtime" was their secret code word. This so-called overtime involved her reporting to the director's tastefully furnished top-floor office where, under the guise of work, they got to know each other intimately. Hanyi would read the news, delivering another broadcast, and though she was free to invent whatever stories she wanted, she usually stuck to the day's national and international headlines. The director took the work of broadcasting seriously, and if she did her job well, he would be ecstatic. That was the true power of the news.

It took a while to find out what the fuss was about. Hanyi dropped off her mud-stained skirt at the dry cleaner's. Three days later, she went to get it back, and the big story she was expecting landed on her desk. It was major news, because the VIP in town was indeed very important, so important that except when he was touring the provinces, she'd ordinarily only see him on the CCTV News. The story said this great leader was bringing with him a spirit of cultural development, acting with penetrating insight, and offering life-giving, compassionate guidance. Hanyi steeled her concentration before the broadcast and delivered the story in a tone as solemn and sure as that of any CCTV broadcaster. The most extraordinary part was the hint of elation in her expression, as if rejoicing at rain in a drought. It was a moving performance, a masterful show. The truth was that Hanyi saw no real connection between herself and the story, and to deliver it this way was a matter of technique, not passion. She left the studio with a sense of accomplishment, and as she reflected in detail on the broadcast, it struck her that though her performance was impeccable, there was still something missing. She washed off her makeup and sat for a while in thought before realizing what it was: each time there was a particularly big story, the director would give it special emphasis, encouraging her before the broadcast and praising her afterward, but this time he hadn't. On the news screen, Hanyi had caught a glimpse of the director, just a brief flash, and she hadn't seen anything unusual, but his absence before and after the broadcast was indeed a strange sign.

For the last two years, rumors had been flying of the director either being promoted or resigning. A promotion meant he'd be transferred to China Media Group, the main state media company, or to an office position, but if he didn't get promoted, he would probably end up retiring because of his age. The rumors flew behind the scenes, but no one talked of it openly. As always, the hot topics at the office were sex, health, and beauty. Two days ago, when the director had summoned her, she had seen no sign of anything strange. They were putting their clothes back on when Hanyi mentioned she'd seen Xiabo at the plastic surgeon's office, and the director chuckled amicably. "Ah, the bravery of the young, always striving to get ahead!" This comment rubbed Hanyi the wrong way, and she sneered, "Why don't you get plastic surgery too?" This caught him off guard, and he furrowed his brow. "Are you saying I'm ugly? Do you think I'm old?" His pitch rose on the last word, "old," as if offended by the very suggestion. Not missing a beat, Hanyi replied, "You'll only have to go in twice, for silicon tits and Botox in the butt." She stood, putting one hand on her chest and one on her rear, so that her body formed an *s* shape, and said, "That way you can grope yourself anytime you want." After a stunned pause, the director burst out laughing. Laughing roused him, encouraged him, "promoting" him back to high spirits.

The station had no shortage of gossip hounds. They had been quite talkative over the past two days, but Hanyi remained discreet. Outside of broadcasts, her mouth mostly stayed closed, but with the headset off, she kept her ears wide open. The source of the information was unclear, and it was confused and conflicted, but the gist of it was that the director's final days were near. His cavalier, careless approach to important stories seemed to confirm it. Theoretically, only a few people should have known, but if word had reached the head of the news division, that meant it was common knowledge. For most people a meeting with the station director was hard to come by, so they had no way to confirm it for themselves, but as far as they could tell from observing his confidante Hanyi, nothing seemed out of place.

Being a close confidante of the director meant exactly what it implied. Hanyi knew that well. She'd never liked the director, but she'd never pushed him away. For the past two days, though, she'd been distracted. As she sat there, she had the nagging sensation of a hand groping her, and she only stopped herself from squirming through sheer willpower. But squirming in her seat was the least of her problems. During the broadcast of *On Air*, she tripped over her tongue, but luckily the supposedly live broadcast had more than a ten-minute delay, or she would have been in big trouble. She had managed to get distracted at just the wrong time. The one person who could help her was the director. He enjoyed working with her. He worked hard, working up a sweat, so busy he could barely catch his breath, as she urged him toward ecstasy by reading the news. The national and international news emerged from her crimson lips and sparkling teeth as she puffed and panted. There was no passion at all behind it, but her broadcasts had the intended effect. The director would be roused, excited, filled with vigor... Calling it overtime was not entirely a joke. This overtime was a kind of medicine, and it also affected Hanyi. The first effect was that her position at the anchor's desk was more secure than ever, and the second was that, as she sat before the camera, her attention would sometimes wander. Hanyi was a professional, and she had developed a resistance to this second effect. That is, she hardly ever became self-conscious or stumbled over words during an actual broadcast. If it weren't for all the rumors about the director, she wouldn't have suddenly blushed during the broadcast.

It took effort to avoid the medicine's second effect. It was hard not to stutter when her thoughts turned to the director's strange predilection during the broadcast, just as she at first had trouble fulfilling his requests. Once, when they'd just begun their secret meetings, he had asked her to make more noise, thinking she was bored. Well aware of her strengths, she nonetheless asked with a grin, "What kind of noise? I don't like making noise." Then, as if she'd suddenly realized what he meant, she laughed. "Oh, you want me to scream?" Taken aback, the director laughed and said, "Ah, yes, what I want you to scream is—" Smoothly taking the cue, Hanyi cried softly, "Sex—sex—sex—sex!" She pronounced it in each of the four tones, giving it every possible dipping and diving accent, and the result was an impeccable display of vocal mastery. The director was beside himself with joy, but he said with a straight face, "My god, what a voice. Why waste it on a single syllable?" The director demonstrated what he wanted her to do, and Hanyi could hardly believe her ears. Following his lead, she began a halting, hesitant "repeat broadcast." From then on, she was the keeper of the director's medicine. It left her lips like the alchemical pill of immortality, each syllable a luminous pearl, and no matter how weary the director was from work, he would pull himself together again, lift himself to another climax.

It wasn't that Hanyi was anxious to see the director, but it was true that she was looking forward to meeting him. Just before the end of work that evening, Xiabo arrived at the station wearing a ridiculously oversized pair of sunglasses. If she was concerned about an infection after her surgery, that was her business, but what annoyed Hanyi was that she launched into an enthusiastic poetry recitation: "Ah! Rather than dwell on the cliff for a thousand years, tonight I would lean on my lover's shoulder and cry! Ah!" It was Shu Ting's "Goddess Peak" with two added *ahs*, and Xiabo jiggled her own peaks as she recited the poem. It was a vulgar, over-the-top display, to the accompaniment of a poem about an adulterous tryst. At the moment, Hanyi had yet to meet the station director. Just then, her phone rang—it was her husband. He had gotten in touch with the director, he said, the deal was basically done, and he was leaving right away for Shanghai. Hanyi had an inkling of what was coming. Sure enough, just after the broadcast of *Daily Highlights*, the director called. They arranged a meeting, but this time, rather than the director's office suite, he invited himself to Hanyi's home "for a friendly chat." She understood what the invitation meant, but until now her home had remained virgin territory, a line they had yet to cross. And he was in such an ebullient mood that it implied his situation had stabilized, that life was good again, or maybe he hoped to rekindle the flame between them to take his mind off his troubles—at the moment, there was no way she could know. The last place Hanyi wanted to meet was her home, but she couldn't talk him out of it. When she reached home half an hour later, the director's car was parked in the garage downstairs.

It was an extremely unusual meeting. Hanyi lived in a large, luxurious, single-story condo, nearly 200 square meters, with three bedrooms and four TVs. The four TVs were not signs of Hanyi's vanity or narcissism. In fact, she was not in the habit of watching herself on TV. Her husband had brought home the TVs. As an electrical engineer, he was an expert in the field and passionately interested in new technology. A 3-D TV, the latest model, hung in the living room, and there were two sets of 3-D glasses on the coffee table.

The director sat down on the sofa, picked up a pair of glasses, toyed with them a while, and then put them on. Hanyi had worn the 3-D glasses just a few times, so you could say both pairs were her husband's. She looked at the director, eyes flashing with contempt. The big, white-framed glasses looked ridiculous on him, and they made everything blurry, so that even her contempt was blurred out, and he couldn't see it. Considering his profession, learning about the latest visual technology was all in a day's work, she supposed. He took off the glasses and held them in his hand, squinting with far-sighted eyes, sizing her up. The look made her uncomfortable, so she decided to take him on a tour. He strolled around praising this and agreeing with that before coming to a stop at the bedroom door.

She stepped aside to let him pass, then stepped a bit farther aside to look at herself in the living room mirror. In the mirror, her face was like a lotus, her brow slightly furrowed. She'd planned to make a careful study of his expression, but he had a well-practiced poker face, and she could see nothing, nor did it seem the time to ask questions. She turned on the light by the mirror, saw the fine wrinkles at the corners of her eyes, and couldn't keep her heart from sinking. Suddenly, she heard her own voice. It was another repeat broadcast! The director had turned on the TV in the bedroom. She froze in place. All of a sudden, she had a funny feeling. The eyes of her reflection widened, seeing nothing but herself. The woman on TV was an illusion too. If she turned the other three sets to the same channel, there would be no less than six of her in the house! It was comical but also chilling. She hurriedly turned off the light and stepped away from the mirror before the director could catch sight of her. She knew well what he would do. He would stand behind her, carefully look her over, stretch out his arms, and embrace her.

But she couldn't stop those arms from reaching out. He grabbed her by the hands, pulled her close, and led her to the master bedroom. He had changed in an instant from guest to host. As long as he was here, he was going to take charge, if only temporarily. He thrust himself onto the front lines of battle, charging against the home's key defenses. The commander's post had been left abandoned, and now he was the man of the house. It was a man's nature to seize control. He might not control the whole building, but at least this room was his. Having plotted his strategy and staked his claim, he put no thought into what happened next. Truly being master meant doing what you pleased, and today he had his mind set to act on his urges.

He reclined at the head of the bed, but Hanyi did not come, and she did not speak. She was an intelligent woman, and she knew that if she asked nothing, he would not speak either. She sat down in the armchair, picked up the remote, changed the channel on herself, and flipped randomly through the stations. The screen flashed and darkened again and again. There was a girl on a stage making an exaggeratedly cute face, then, suddenly, an image of a wedding; a wedding march sounded briefly, then changed to a funeral dirge. Now a funeral scene was onscreen. Hanyi hit mute. On the silent screen, a man stood on a platform giving an address, his mouth snapping open and shut, arms gesturing wildly. Hanyi smiled through pursed lips, and with another flick of the finger, she changed the channel to a legal program. One set of hands placed another in cuffs. A microphone thrust onto the screen, pointing at a tear-streaked face.

Hanyi turned the sound back on. The downcast mouth delivered a blubbery, barely coherent confession, but it was clear what the crime was. Hanyi snuck a glance at the director. Reclining in bed, he looked perfectly comfortable, and she saw no sign of emotion. He stirred a little and pointed to the round end table. There was another remote there, the one for the air conditioner. Hanyi turned on the air conditioner, waved the director away, and dialed her husband's cellphone.

After less than a minute, she hung up. His voice had been barely audible over all the noise, the most reassuring noise imaginable. Any other background sound would have left some doubt, but the rumbling of the high-speed train eased her mind. The air-conditioning was kicking in, and the room's atmosphere had turned suggestive. She put down the cellphone and lowered her eyes. Without looking at the director, she began taking off her clothes. She had a graceful figure and breasts like plump, juicy berries. It looked as if warm syrup would ooze out at the slightest touch, but as always, these fruits hung high on the branch. That is, she simply sat without moving a muscle. The director rose and came toward her.

What happened next was as easy as water flowing downstream. Only because it was an exceptional time, because of all the rumors, had she agreed reluctantly to meet him in this exceptional place. She had yet to learn anything. Even when news of the corrupt official's arrest came on the TV, he wasn't at all moved. He was world-wise, impossible to read. Hanyi simply relaxed and let him do as he pleased. She even encouraged him a little. When they were about to really get started, it was clear the director could not perform. He paused a moment, then said, "Begin."

Hanyi understood that she was to begin the broadcast. Rather than millions of TV sets, this broadcast would be transmitted to one man alone. He would accompany her in this performance. Today, suddenly, Hanyi was not in the mood to talk. "Oh," she said, reaching for the remote control. She randomly pressed some buttons and quickly came upon the repeat broadcast of *On Air.* She turned up the volume, and the room filled at once with the sound of her voice. She planned to have the TV broadcast do the work for her. She had used this trick before, but today the director wouldn't let it pass. Holding Hanyi's inquiring gaze, he insisted, "Begin, now!"

There was nothing she could do but steel her concentration, draw a breath, and start in on the task. It felt so strange being here in her own bed, so far from the station building. She stammered, and she panted, unlike the Hanyi on the TV. The Hanyi on TV was the teacher, and the Hanyi in bed was the student. It was a fascinating contrast, and this strange spectacle stirred the director's passion for his work, until it was as strong as a gale-force wind, hard as driving rain, powerful as the pounding surf. Hanyi's words wouldn't form sentences, as if the wind had blown them to bits, scattering the sheets with punctuation marks. She breathed in deeply and, suddenly inspired, cast away the script provided by the TV and began a totally improvised broadcast.

She didn't always use a script on *Daily Highlights.* Sometimes the director overworked himself during the day, collapsing from fatigue in the evening. At times like this, he would hand her a reputable newspaper, and she would scan the main stories and deliver the broadcast without a script. He said he was testing Hanyi's ability to adapt. The more important the story, and the more famous the figures involved, the greater his passion. It was as if such stories had a magical revitalizing power. Today, nearly without thinking, Hanyi did the opposite, drawing inspiration from the story of the corrupt official on TV. She pondered for a moment and invented a story of a corrupt bureaucrat dismissed from his post. With all the severity and righteousness she could muster, she told of the official being "immediately relieved of his duties." The director froze for a moment, then deflated.

The director looked down on her, catching his breath. After quite some time, he lifted his head and offered his appraisal: "Nice try, but that's not how it happened." Hanyi had simply been making up the story as she went. In the first part of the story the protagonist's name was John Doe, but when she told of his dismissal from duty, she changed the name inadvertently to Jane Doe. The director said, "He deserves a lot worse than getting fired on the spot!" Meeting Hanyi's inquiring gaze, the director described the new story he wanted her to tell: "It was so-and-so! He took bribes and promoted his cronies. He's the one who should be fired and dragged into court!" Hanyi's eyes grew even wider. So-and-so was the highest official in the province, one with the power to hire and fire the station director, for instance, and this request from him struck her as especially strange. Hanyi felt disoriented and afraid. But the director urged good-humoredly, "Your turn!" He elbowed her. She had to begin the broadcast. She tripped over the words. Now her lovely lips were not so nimble. She was unable to state the concrete details of so-and-so's crime, which unintentionally made the broadcast all the more authentic, as this was usually the case with stories of corruption by high officials. But she delivered this last sentence fluidly: "The institutions of justice will investigate the matter and bring resolution." In a split second, the director was filled with vigor, like river rapids rushing through the mountains, sending up spray. He mumbled, "I'll XXXX you to death! I'll XXXX you to death!..." The sentence was short, but the subject, object, and verb were all there, clear and complete. "Crashing straight down three thousand feet, like the Milky Way falling from the heavens"—so went the poem by Li Bai. As he climaxed, it was as if the rain ceased and the clouds parted, and before his eyes he saw stars.

Much later, having changed into a fresh set of clothes, Hanyi sat on the sofa staring into space. She was alone. The washing machine rumbled, the bedsheets inside tangled like the thoughts in her head. It seemed the director's powers of persuasion still held, or at least, they wouldn't give way right away. He'd once insisted, if a government leader does something and we don't report it, then in one sense they never did it! Hanyi stood, walked to the TV in the master bedroom, and inspected it carefully. It was off, and the screen was black. She bent down, reached behind, felt for the cable, and pulled it out. Then she went to the small bedroom where her husband slept, and turned on the computer. She hadn't installed any of the equipment. It was her husband's handiwork, but she'd been on guard against something like this. It didn't take long to find the file she was looking for. She copied it to a flash drive and wiped it from the hard drive.

The TV in the little bedroom was black, too. There was nothing on the screen, no dirty video playing. She slipped the flash drive into her purse. Now it was in her hands alone. Like all men and women who make such videos, she was sure it would remain forever in her hands.

The Elephant

大象

Chan Chi Wa
Translated by Audrey Heijns

街角有道士在作法求雨，揮舞一把雨傘，口中唸唸有詞。

"There was a Taoist priest on the corner of the street praying for rain, waving an umbrella, chanting incantations."

After the elephant vanished, my life fell into chaos. Strange things happened during that extremely dry summer. It was the kind of drought that O City experienced only once in a century. Many water reservoirs had dried up and drinking water was in short supply, while asphalt roads were full of cracks and trees began to wither. Sweat evaporated as soon as it passed through the skin and people had a thin layer of salt on their faces and backs. Residents complained bitterly and everywhere there were cries of discontent. Officials of O City took turns on television asking for patience. For several days in a row the missing elephant made the headlines in the newspaper, including: "Disappearance of Elephant Damages Popular Trust in the System" and "Matter of Elephant Adversely Affects Public Opinion of the Government." As a result, the government of O City had no choice but to take the matter of the missing elephant seriously. Everywhere in the street, police not only put up posters with advice on how to use water sparingly but also notices asking the public for leads. All kinds of rumors about the elephant started to spread in the streets, such as that it had been buried hastily by authorities in an attempt to cover up its horrible death from extreme dehydration. My husband Apat said that there was another even more bizarre version saying that the elephant had succumbed to the drought and melted like ice cream, turned into a heap of salt on weeds. Nobody knew what had really happened. I could have regarded the incident as merely a topic for small talk over tea, just like all other citizens of O City. However, on the fourth day after the disappearance of the elephant was made known in the news, two policemen came knocking at my door. I was asked to come to the police station for interrogation.

The tall constable pulled a photo from his pocket and placed it in front of me. "Miss Yip Yau Yau, do you know who this is?" I recognized him immediately. The man in the photo was Ting Wai Ming. He had been my classmate when I was studying in V City. I knew that he had come to the park in O City especially to see the elephant. Several years ago, the park had been built in the suburbs of O City to stimulate the economy. The world's largest tent was built, and the most famous circus was invited to O City from abroad to perform in the tent and attract tourists to come and see the show. The government even bought an expensive elephant. I did not personally go and see the elephant, but I saw what it looked like on TV and in newspapers. Many people from afar came to see the elephant; Ting Wai Ming was one of them. The tall policeman told me that on the day that the elephant disappeared Ting Wai Ming had been seen near the park. And then Ting Wai Ming had also vanished. His luggage was still in the hotel and he had not checked out. There was also no departure record indicating that he had left the country. They found out that the last call he had made from the room was my cellphone number. In fact, the day Ting called me, he only told me that he had finally seen the elephant, but it was all dried up and much smaller than he had imagined. I said it was probably the dry weather that must have affected its appetite. Then I heard him sigh before he hung up. I relayed this conversation to the officer exactly how it had been, but he only frowned. He asked me if I was sure that I had told him everything, if I had not omitted anything. I had no other choice but to repeat the conversation again. Eventually they made me sign a written statement that was full of spelling mistakes and urged me to notify them immediately should I hear from Ting Wai Ming. Then they let me go home.

However, my life fell into chaos. From then onward it felt as if I were being followed. In the streets, where normally nobody was about, there were strangers who circled around me front and back, and often there was a strange static on my cellphone. When I told Apat that I was being followed, he laughed at me and said I had read too many detective stories. The headlines in the newspapers were still about the elephant, including "Who Stole Our Elephant?" and "Police Offer Reward for Finding Elephant." I stared at my computer screen to watch the news until my eyes began to hurt, and I tried to find eyedrops. While I searched in vain, I happened to come across a notebook with Apat's handwriting on the cover. It had daily records of the times that I went out and came home. I didn't know why he had made records of that, and I wondered if I should ask him for an explanation. Maybe it was only a weird habit of his. We had been married for five years, but I had never realized he had such a weird habit. I could not find any eyedrops, so I went out to buy them. The dry weather was really unbearable; my lips were so dry all the time that, when I touched them with my tongue, I tasted blood. My skin was so itchy it was unbearable; I had to apply lotion to my face and body all the time. There was a Taoist priest on the corner of the street praying for rain, waving an umbrella, chanting incantations. I walked along the street to the pharmacy that I usually go to. The price of eyedrops had gone up again. While I was walking down the street, I had this extraordinary feeling that I resembled a withered leaf. The bottle of water that I had brought with me was empty. Therefore, I went to find shelter in a coffee shop along the road.

The jukebox in the coffee shop was playing a song. It was a female voice that sang slowly, "It was me and a gun, and a man on my back..." I turned my head away and looked at the wizened tree outside, when I saw Apat stealthily coming out of the building on the opposite side of the street, followed by the tall policeman. They looked at each other and then parted company. I quickly put some eyedrops in my eyes, which must have blurred my vision. I wondered if I was hallucinating—the scene in front of me must have been an illusion, a misconception, a mirage in broad daylight. I blinked and they were already far away. When I returned home, Apat was watching TV in the living room. It was the new model that we had bought in installments last year. People on the screen were talking, but the voice of the song in the coffee shop was still stuck in my head, unwilling to go. In order to dispel my suspicion, I planned to put Apat to the test. I input an appointment in the calendar app of my phone: *Wai Ming, Fai Lok Restaurant, Fok Man Road, 8 pm.* I left my phone on the side table on purpose and told Apat that I was meeting a friend for dinner that night. I went to the bathroom, staring blankly and breathing in the mirror. Just as I was about to write something on the mirror, the vapor cleared. I changed and went out. I went to Fai Lok restaurant alone. I pushed open the door of the restaurant and saw a reproduction by Bacon, hanging high on the wall. It was Pope Innocent X with his hideous face, mouth open in terror, as if screaming silently at the patrons of the restaurant. I was wondering if this was a new way to stimulate our appetite. The waiter served me a steak that was dripping blood. While I was chewing my steak, I rejoiced that my test had failed. No policeman came to disturb me during dinner and I had no reason to suspect Apat. It must have been the arid conditions that had let my imagination run wild.

I paid the bill and was about to leave when I saw that, to my surprise, it was pouring rain outside. Actually, nobody had expected it would rain. People sought shelter from the rain under the eaves of the restaurant. They were confused and excited at the same time. Everyone was talking and making all sorts of comments. There were even some people running around and cheering in the rain. One man was so shocked by the rain that he stood with his mouth open, a spitting image of Pope Innocent X in the painting on the wall. I looked back at Bacon's reproduction, but I only saw the tall policeman. He gave a nod in greeting and said in a dull tone: "It's raining, at last."

Raindrops splashed, hitting the cracks in the road ferociously. We watched the rain for I don't know how long, when

I finally plucked up the courage to ask: "Have you been following me?" He remained quiet for a long time, until he said: "I thought I would see Ting Wai Ming. I did not expect to see rain." I said: "It was an elephant. Did you really think Ting Wai Ming would steal it? And where could he have hidden it?" He pulled a book from his backpack. It was a collection of Japanese short stories. He said: "This author describes the disappearance of an elephant and his keeper. It also mentions that for some unfathomable reason the body of the elephant kept on shrinking. We think that Ting Wai Ming is involved. Therefore, we must find him." I said: "But that is fiction…" He retorted: "Don't they say that truth is stranger than fiction?"

With the end of the dry weather, O City recovered its vitality. The news headlines reported: "Finally Rainfall. Authorities Are Happy to See That Public Opinion Has Gone Up Again." To celebrate the event, there were fireworks displays in the harbor of O City for several days in a row. They also ordered a couple of specially made robot elephants for the park in the suburbs. They were remarkably true to life. They even imitated the sounds of elephants, while their ears, tails, and trunks could also move. As before, local residents and tourists alike flocked in masses to see them. Apat was still my husband, but between us some things had melted like soft serve, impossible to describe. Yet because of financial considerations, we still continued to play the role of a married couple. And I was still happy to go to Fai Lok restaurant alone and have my steak. I cut the steak and blood slowly seeped out. Outside it was drizzling, moss was growing in the gutter that had once been dried up. On the wall of the restaurant, Pope Innocent X was still hanging with his mouth open. I looked at him for a very long time until my eyes hurt, and then I put eyedrops in. They stopped following me, which felt strange in the beginning, as if life were lacking something. There was no longer anybody concerned about the whereabouts of the elephant or Ting Wai Ming. I remember people saying that the elephant didn't stop shrinking, but to me it had never shrunk; on the contrary it was growing larger. Both the elephant and Ting Wai Ming were getting larger. They became so large that I couldn't see them anymore, and I was forever living in their shadows.

The Mushroom Houses Proliferated in District M

香菇屋在M區盛放

Enoch Tam
Translated by Jeremy Tiang

香菇自會在雨天吸水，縮在碩大的菇頂裏，只要把水龍頭駁到菇頂處，水就會源源不絕的流下來。

"The mushrooms absorbed rain, storing it in their enormous caps. All you had to do was connect a faucet to the ceiling, and water would gurgle down."

It was the garden-keepers who ruined the mushrooms.

A decade ago, they started growing mushrooms in District N. Before this, mushrooms had been the crop of ordinary people. There was no need for the garden-keepers, with all their influence and resources, to soil their hands with such unprofitable work, but they wanted a finger in every pie. Business owners played along to stay on their good side, and even regular folk had no choice but to buy their mushrooms. Not because these were particularly fresh or tasty but because they were so huge—big enough to live in. Their roots reached deep into the earth, and neither wind nor rain could knock them over. The garden-keepers hollowed out these ginormous mushrooms, installed doors and windows in the stems, then sold them off according to size.

Very soon, the garden-keepers had cornered the market in mushrooms.

Others tried to emulate them but, without access to their techniques, could only produce mushrooms fit for eating. Property developers continued building boxes for people to live in, which of course were not as profitable as the mushrooms. Still, business was business, and the poorer people of City H who couldn't afford mushrooms were reduced to these box dwellings, which may have been boringly square, their walls inelastic and their interiors lacking natural aromas, but at least they were sufficient protection from the elements that a human being could settle down to a more or less stable life. The main problem was they lacked roots, which meant they couldn't grip the ground. From time to time, the wind would blow them long distances. Some genius thought of linking these boxes with metal chains. This did indeed make them less prone to movement, and only once every few years would a storm be strong enough that you'd see, if you were watching from a high-rise balcony, a row of eight or ten houses chained together, slinking their way down the street like a military convoy through a hail of bullets, swerving randomly this way and that, following the wind wherever the wind wanted to go. When the residents opened their front doors the morning after the storm, they'd find their street completely transformed, a seafood restaurant suddenly where a convenience store used to be, a stationery store now replaced by a comic book shop. Still, being used to this reshuffle taking place once every few years, they simply got dressed as usual and went off to work.

But the garden-keepers ruined the mushrooms in District M.

When they first started growing mushrooms, it was with the intention of bringing a new lifestyle and form of housing into City H. Being plants, mushrooms would continue growing as long as they were able to absorb adequate nutrition. Some of the garden-keepers' mushrooms produced little offshoots, which in time grew large enough to be turned into additional rooms. Not every mushroom spawned in this way, though—it was entirely buyer's luck. Either way, the mushroom houses were first-rate residences. Inside, they were filled with an earthy, fungal fragrance, and being able to breathe, they could regulate their internal temperature to a comfortable twenty-two to twenty-five degrees Celsius. The people of H couldn't have asked for better accommodation. If they wanted to change the layout of their dwellings, there was no need to tear down or build walls; they simply had to set down some fertilizer in the right place and water it, and a wall would sprout there the next day. The garden-keepers bragged that the mushroom houses were completely natural and therefore would have the lowest impact on the local ecosystem. These dwellings processed everything from food waste to sewage. As for running water, that was no problem either. The mushrooms absorbed rain, storing it in their enormous caps. All you had to do was connect a faucet to the ceiling, and water would gurgle down. Even more importantly, as eco-technology advanced, it became possible to modify these natural features according to the customer's wishes. For instance, a northerner might find twenty-two degrees too warm and could request a genetically modified mushroom with a lower temperature. Apparently, these could be as cool as eighteen or even fifteen degrees.

Then they started planting mushrooms in District M.

In District N, the garden-keepers had firm restrictions to keep the mushroom houses from growing too closely together. This was partly out of fear that the mushrooms would crowd or even damage each other as they got larger, requiring the garden-keepers to pay compensation, and partly because they weren't sure if the land would have enough nutrients. Not wanting to lay down fertilizer with too heavy a hand, they'd appointed experts to survey the soil and adjusted the mushroom density accordingly. When it came to District M, however, all their caution went out the window. As soon as a buyer placed an order, they'd plant another mushroom. Rumor had it they'd made losses on their other businesses and were rushing to turn a profit here. The mushrooms proliferated in District M, and although it wasn't so bad that they actually touched, there were indeed not enough nutrients in the ground to feed them all. They began dying off soon after reaching maturity, turning into blackened stumps. The residents of District M found that their houses suddenly stopped growing and could no longer regulate their internal temperature, never mind sprouting internal walls or providing running water. They didn't smell so good either. The streets of District M gradually became lined with these misshapen fungi, but the garden-keepers didn't dare take responsibility, so instead they pushed the blame onto the agricultural company they'd contracted to till the soil, insisting they must have leached out the fertility as they ploughed.

With the mushrooms no longer habitable, many property owners moved elsewhere, and the garden-keepers allowed them to mortgage their mushrooms so they could afford temporary boxes to live in. The ruined mushrooms were remodeled to provide all manner of retail opportunities. People could donate portions of their bodies to provide a day's nutrients for a mushroom. For that day, the donor would be allowed to live in that mushroom. Stomach muscles were particularly coveted; toned men and women could hand over this stored energy to power the mushrooms, receiving a bellyful of blubber in return. In order to experience life in a mushroom house for a day, quite a few people handed over their six-packs or other parts of their anatomy. The garden-keepers then siphoned off a portion of the energy and nutrients, transferring it to the now-depleted District N. As a result, the mushroom houses of District N grew more resplendent than ever, even as M's stock dwindled.

As for the residents who refused to move out of M, they asked the government to rebuild their houses so they'd have somewhere to live. The government had no choice but to construct some old-style boxes for them. Eventually though, they gave up and got some experts to declare that District M was full of toxins from the decomposing mushrooms and no longer fit for human habitation. They urged the remaining residents to leave voluntarily, before they got forcibly removed. The next morning, the recalcitrants woke up to find their mushroom houses had been plucked up by the roots and transplanted to District S. When they looked out, there was suddenly a seafood restaurant where a convenience store used to be, a stationery store replaced by a comic book shop. Still, being used to this reshuffle taking place once every few years, they simply got dressed as usual and went off to work.

A Counterfeit Life

冒牌人生

Chen Si'an

Translated by Canaan Morse

日復一日，他們倆好像兩顆漂浮在這個城市污濁空氣中的顆粒物，隱形又無處不在。

"Day after day, they floated like two molecules of smog in this city's densely polluted air, totally invisible and everywhere at once."

"So, what I'm saying is: Most people come here in order to live. But I feel like I'm going to be here till I die."

The moment he slowed down he felt the cold. The moment he felt the cold, his brain turned back on. The moment his brain turned back on, that sentence floated back into his ear. He couldn't for the life of him remember where he'd first read it.

It really was cold in this city. Piercing whiteness stretched along the ground in all directions, except for the dirtied places where people walked.

One more company. Probably no luck there either, he thought. Shivering fingers fished a pack of cigarettes from his pocket; shivering hands held a lighter to his face; shivering lips sucked in a mouthful of smoke. His threadbare, charcoal-gray Western suit provided no insulation at all, its fabric flapping and rattling in the wind as if it were paper. He'd bought it for a couple hundred yuan right after graduation, figuring he didn't need to spend too much just to get through a couple of interviews. He never expected he'd be putting it on daily from summer all the way to winter, then through a second summer and far into yet another winter.

He watched people in white-collar outfits stream out of an office building, observing how and by what paths they navigated the snowy ground. This one strides proudly along the approved pedestrian walkway straight into one muddy slush puddle after another. This one hops like a stork between patches of dry ground, jumping clear across the mud puddle only to land on a thin sheet of ice that drops him into icy water. Another one shuffles forward with tentative baby steps until the people accumulating behind her get frustrated enough to push right past her.

Sigh. Obviously, all people with a spare pair of shoes.

He dropped his cigarette, which hissed in the snow. Got to move around some, or his bones would freeze brittle.

Move where? Some place with easier walking.

Looking around, he noticed that the owners of the first-floor shops had each shoveled out the patch of curb in front of his or her own door, thereby clearing a pathway. He stomped his feet a few times and started to pace down this clean avenue that might disappear at any moment.

So, if everybody else felt like moving here had allowed

them to really live, why did everything he set his heart on always die? That said, since everything he wanted always died, why should he keep hanging on here? He felt a cold draught between his toes and looked down at his shoe. He'd stepped in slush while jostling his way out of the subway station that morning, and the fake leather had soaked through instantaneously. Yet another piece of it had flaked off at some point between then and now. His pace slowed as he stared at the shoe, until he had stopped completely.

Once again, shivering fingers plucked out a cigarette, shivering fingers raised the lighter, shivering lips drew in mouthfuls of smoke. He waited for more people to appear on the street. He liked to stand on the curb and watch others pass by, watch how they talked, walked, and treated each other. If only there were some job that let you stand outside and watch people for money.

So many people went through hell and high water every day in this place—it was fascinating. Frigid wind had harassed his back into a state of constant shivering; his spine made popping noises as the flesh twitched. He twisted his trunk and shook himself. His fingers could barely keep hold of the cigarette. Just stand for a while longer, just for a bit. His cigarette was almost cashed out; he sucked it a little more gently.

"Hey! We've been waiting for you forever! Where the hell

did you go? Hey! Hello?" A man in a black tuxedo and a buzz cut emerged from one of the storefronts he was standing near and hurried toward him.

The sudden shout startled him, and he simply stared at the man with the buzz cut. The other man stared back. Their gazes met, and for a moment neither knew quite what to do.

"It is you, yeah?" The man lowered his cellphone and asked in a tone of voice so loaded with impatience and aggression that it felt like a response in the negative would earn him a slap in the face.

"Hmm." The pitch of his voice rose at the beginning of the syllable like he was asking a question, then fell into an affirmative. It was a habitual verbal affectation of his that made his speech seem light and hard to pin down.

Buzz-cut breathed a sigh of relief as he turned off his cellphone and stuffed it in his pocket. The tension between the two men relaxed significantly.

"We've been tearing our hair out waiting for you, look at the time already. And you're out here taking a smoke break? Get in there, let's go. After it's all over, I'll send you a couple cartons and you can smoke as slowly as you want." Buzz-cut started pushing him toward the door, and the burning butt of his cigarette fell from between his numb fingers onto the snow. A second shove forced him off his footing, and he followed Buzz-cut into the store.

"Hmm." Another syllable that began as a question and ended as an answer.

While Buzz-cut dragged him inside, he whispered in his ear: "Both sets of parents are cultured types, they don't want anything too loud or gaudy, so you don't have to do the whole circus ringmaster thing, all right? Just step-by-step, beginning to end, and that's it. No stunts and no funny business, just festive and dignified. Remember that: festive and dignified."

When the door opened, a burst of warm air hit him in the face and he felt like a frozen fish dropped in a bucket of hot water. His skin warmed immediately, even as the cold still clung to his innards and spine.

"Okay, okay, the emcee's finally here! Let's go, everyone, the lucky hour's almost over. Get the bride and groom and the parents into their seats. Okay, we're starting now, we're starting!" Buzz-cut dragged him into the banquet hall to the edge of a small stage decorated with plastic floral wreaths and carpeted in red. He shoved a wireless microphone into his hands.

"Don't forget: *festive* and *dignified*." Buzz-cut switched on the microphone.

With the microphone in hand, he looked around the banquet hall. He counted a dozen or so tables of food and drink, each ringed with guests, who were laughing and talking exuberantly, making a boisterous mess of light and noise that filled every corner of the room. No one paid any attention to what was happening on the stage.

"Get up there, man, what are you waiting for?" Buzz-cut jabbed a finger into his ribs.

"I, ah..." He hesitated. I'm not an emcee, he wanted to say, but even those four words wouldn't come out. Even in the moment of his hesitation, he had no idea what he was hesitating for.

"What is it, the money? For heaven's sake. I'll pay you right after it's all over, promise I won't make you wait. Get it in gear, man, if the lucky hour passes by, then I'm in trouble." Buzz-cut poked him once more in the ribs; seeing that he was still unsure, he pushed him straight onstage.

He looked out once more at the banquet audience. As before, no one was paying any attention to him. He had been to plenty of weddings himself, and he basically knew how they went. Might as well give it a shot, he thought, nobody was really looking at him anyway, and he had seen it all before.

He gently cleared his throat and raised the microphone to his lips. "Honored guests, friends and family, welcome one and all to this festive and dignified ceremony... This is the world of flowers, this is the ocean of love, this is a wedding hall brimful of happiness..."

Everything proceeded much more quickly than he had expected. By the time the entire ceremony ended (the whole thing took less than a quarter of an hour), he had only just started to feel warm. In fact, his forehead pulsed with heat and his sweat-soaked shirt clung to his back.

At more than one point he had found himself so lost for words he thought he would surely be discovered. The best he could do was stand onstage and invite the bride and groom to drink a champagne toast, then cut the cake, then toast each other once more. Yet in those moments he discovered that nobody really cared that much about the ritual. No one tried to kick him out or micromanage him; no one criticized his clumsy directions or called him out on his anemic stage presence.

His astonishment was so great it overcame the physical tension of anxiety.

He concluded the slapdash ceremony with a string of formulaic, greeting-card blessings, and the banquet hall immediately recovered its energetic atmosphere. He turned and stepped offstage. The man with the buzz cut took the microphone from him and switched it off. Without raising his eyes, Buzz-cut asked: "Well? You gonna stick around for lunch?"

"No, sorry. I've got things to do."

Buzz-cut looked him over for a moment, then snorted. "I figured you were in a hurry to get to another event. Why else would you have cut so many corners for us here?"

That was it; they had figured him out. His body tensed, and he stood in awkward silence, unable to respond.

Buzz-cut reached into his pocket and pulled out a wad of hundreds, peeled a few off, and handed them to him. "Don't complain about the fee. You only deserve this much for a performance like that, let alone for coming so late. I have to take some off the top just to teach you a lesson. Remember: you work one of my weddings, you can't do a careless job." He murmured an apology and took the cash. Buzz-cut turned to leave, then paused as if he'd just remembered something. He pulled a pack of wedding cigarettes out of his other pocket and passed it to him.

He walked out of the hotel back to the spot where he had been standing a half hour before, tore the pack of cigarettes open, and lit up. He took several deep pulls and exhaled. He stood for a long moment, not feeling the cold.

It was like all these people had no idea who or what they were waiting for and didn't really care who eventually showed up. Perhaps "who" wasn't that important to the people waiting, as long as they got someone. And perhaps the expectations of the people waiting weren't that crucial in the eyes of the people being waited for. *And then there is me. I wasn't the one they were waiting for, but I showed up, so what should I think of this whole thing?* He pondered this uncanny situation as he watched the flow of people.

He thought of the real emcee, the one who never showed. Why hadn't he come? Maybe he picked up more important work at the last minute. Maybe after leaving his house, he discovered the iron had burned a hole in his tux. Maybe the traffic was so bad it put him in a foul mood and he went home. Or maybe he just woke up on the wrong side of the bed that morning and decided not to come.

No matter what the reason was that kept the real emcee from appearing, it had changed the course of his life forever.

He started roaming around every corner of the city, searching for those spots in which people being waited for might fail to show up. At first, his inexperience led people to suspect him, and sometimes even figure him out; and on a few occasions, the real person showed up and unmasked his charade. Yet in most cases, he successfully took control of the situation, and he grew gradually more familiar with the problems he had to solve.

The least challenging and most profitable of these situations were the large-scale meetings and banquets. After some trial and error, he discovered that the larger the organization, the more likely it was that most employees had never met each other before; the larger the meeting, the greater the number of empty seats would be. All he needed to do was wait by the entryway of a hotel or meeting room until the moment came when he could step into the flow of arriving guests and get inside. Most of the time, there wasn't even a sign-in sheet, but even when there was one, he simply made up a name on the spot, since no one actually checked the list. After the meeting was over, he could follow the crowd to the dining room of some restaurant and enjoy a free, sumptuous lunch or dinner. Some meetings came with souvenirs or gifts. Once he got good enough, he was able to join the crowd right before the meal and skip the excruciating experience of sitting through a meeting.

It turned out that anyone with a pulse could do jobs like these. They required no technical skill; you simply had to be reasonably well-dressed and uncommunicative. Wedding and funeral receptions, annual company parties, and the like also fell into this category. Thus, once he had satisfied his initial appetite and curiosity, he lost interest in such jobs, unless he was in the right mood or felt like improving his diet.

Otherwise, he followed his interests toward more challenging tasks, like working himself into small-scale meetings, in which there was even a chance he himself might be expected to speak. When the meeting topic was foreign to him, he let his instincts lead him from one empty generalization to another.

When the topic was of interest to him, he often came forth with a whole series of ideas and suggestions.

Later, he began challenging himself to assume any role whenever someone mistook him for someone else. He found that it happened far more often than he would have believed. Most people had absolutely no idea what sort of person they were waiting for.

In order to better acquire different types of "work," he equipped himself with a variety of new outfits and accessories. When he wore his blue coveralls and carried a toolbox, the world consistently mistook him for an electrician or a mechanic. Black slacks and a white collared shirt led them to take him for a real estate agent or a restaurant floor manager. It wasn't classism on their part, they just couldn't be bothered to think twice about it. Before long, he also found out that he had first been mistaken for a wedding emcee because of the red necktie he had paired with his wrinkled gray suit.

He felt at home within any identity and replied to every random stranger who flagged him down with *mm-hmms* and *uh-huhs*. Then he followed these strangers, each desperately in need of someone though they knew not who, into their offices, social spaces, and entertainment halls—even into their homes. When faced with the issues they expected him to solve, he found to his astonishment that a little fiddling around was usually enough to put things right again. People seemed to overestimate the difficulty of every problem and put too much faith in the capability of so-called professionals in that area.

He woke up every morning with no idea of what would happen to him that day—what kind of "work" he would do, where he would end up, what role he would play. The uncertainty excited and encouraged him. His heart filled with new hopes for his future, an emotional state he had never experienced before this point.

Nearly a year after that first serendipitous experience as a wedding emcee, he was living very well—better, one could say, than at any other time in his life. Were one to ask if he had figured anything out, he could say he at least understood this much: the commandment "You need to have a stable and respectable job in order to be happy," which had been force-fed to him for the first twenty-plus years of his life, was false.

Everyone believed that a person needed a solid, reliable "position" to confirm his own existence—a relatively constant "position" in a constantly changing world, a "position" that no one else could assume just as easily. But what about the people who didn't want such a position—they should be allowed to live, too. Over the past year, he had had many opportunities to build a chance encounter into a stable "position," yet he recognized with increasing clarity that such was exactly what he did not want.

One could say that the only regret he had about his current lifestyle was that he held one burning urge which he could not satisfy, namely, the desire to share his understanding of life with other people. Analyzing it in a dispassionate moment, he concluded that it must originate either from the intense human desire to share for the sake of sharing, or from a personal need to prove himself right. And if all he wanted was to prove his ideas correct, that made him no different from anyone else. But since dispassion is not a habitual emotional state for a person, the desire regularly tormented him.

All desires and urges find an opening eventually. His was no exception.

He picked up #2 in front of an office building, the same kind of place where he would eventually find #3, #4, and #5, all the way up to #9. It really was easy for people to connect with others who shared their experience, he later reflected, and even establish trust and an enigmatic feeling of kinship.

He observed #2 for a long time before approaching him. As he watched, he registered a silent amazement at how closely #2 resembled himself from a year ago: shivering violently in the cold as he smoked a cigarette, his gaze unfocused and his jaw set. Even the cheap suit on #2's body looked a lot like the one he used to wear. The sole difference was that #2 carried a plastic pocket folder stuffed with papers under one arm—surely filled, he could imagine, with employment ads from unregistered companies and a sheaf of #2's résumés.

At first, he felt unsure about whether or not he was doing the right thing. In those moments when he agonized over the need to share his life with others, he weighed all potential risks and benefits of such a decision, including the possibility that it might alter or destroy this new life that suited him so well. Yet as soon as he saw the desperation seeping outward from the young man's gaze, saw the growing numbness and the slow leaching of vitality from his body, he realized that it had nothing to do with sharing or desire. He had a responsibility.

After #2 finished his cigarette, he didn't move from his spot in front of the office building. It was likely he didn't know where he should go or what he should do next.

He felt that now was the time to say a few words to #2. A year of experience dealing with innumerable strangers had taught him that no one in this city paid much attention to weirdos. If #2 listened to what he had to say, he might be able to change a person's life; if #2 didn't want to listen, he would just be yet another weirdo on these city streets.

He walked over to #2 and pulled a pack of cigarettes from his pocket. Slapping the top of the pack, he plucked one out and offered it over. #2 took the proffered cigarette and lit it without hesitating or showing any emotion. He made no attempt at small talk. What kind of weirdo bothers with pleasantry? He skipped an introduction and began describing his life over the past year between drags on his own cigarette. While it might have seemed like a complicated tale, it really wasn't; he got through the whole thing in the space of one smoke.

The instant he finished, he felt an indescribable relief wash over him. A thin rime of ice had formed on the faint stubble of his upper lip. He wasn't chatty by nature, talking too much made his cheeks sore. Looking at #2's dazed expression, he smiled and reached up to wipe the ice crystals off his face. He asked #2 if he wanted to have a go at it, to try out his way of life.

After about the third sentence, #2 forgot he was smoking. A column of ash crept toward the cigarette butt he had pinched between his index and middle finger. When its weight became too heavy to bear, it collapsed onto the snow.

As one might expect, entry-level training began with the simplest, most efficient procedures. After a couple of five-star hotel banquets, #2 basically got the hang of it. He helped #2 put together a few useful outfits and taught him how to get into the kinds of spaces where he might find incidental work. #2 proved to be a quick study, and it wasn't long before he became capable of finding work on his own.

He was also astonished to learn that #2 was in fact an

animated young man. Compared to his own stubborn reticence, #2 felt like a regular chatterbox. As time went on, he watched #2 become happier, more open, and even more competent at their line of work than he. #2's quick wit and silver tongue made him especially good at jobs that required strong communication skills.

#2 took to roaming around famous tourist attractions and working as a tour guide when people engaged with him. The work fit #2's personality so well and the compensation was so good that he began to suspect #2 was leaning toward settling into it as a stable occupation. While he never communicated this surmise to #2, he couldn't help but feel a shade disappointed. Yet #2 grew sick of tourist attractions not long after and decided to switch up his line of work. To his great satisfaction he sensed that, like him, #2 wanted the lifestyle for its own sake, and not just as a tool for making money.

Things really had evolved differently than he had first imagined—even better than he had imagined, which surprised him. Occasionally he and #2 would get together at some small restaurant after a day's work to eat and drink and talk about what had happened that day. As #2 narrated with performative verve the fantastic events he'd witnessed, he mused—not without sentimentality—that maybe he really had changed a person's life. This young man's character had been pitted and worn out by something and had lost its color, until he came along and helped to polish it until it shone.

A vague but magical feeling of responsibility, of inescapable destiny, settled on his shoulders.

He first met #47 at the all-members monthly meeting. He remembered quite clearly that she wore a sky-blue cotton skirt and a pair of canvas sneakers that had once been brown before age and weather whitened them. #5 had brought her along. #5 was also female, the first woman he had ever trained. Though he had paid no special attention to gender distribution after #5 joined, he did notice that her presence did attract more female colleagues to the group.

#5 led #47 over and pointed to him, saying: “This is #1. Everything started with him.” Then she turned to him and gestured to #47 with her eyes. “This is #47. I've already checked with the others, the number is open.”

He looked at #47 and she looked back at him. She didn't seem at all nervous or excited by his presence the way many of the others had been. She simply looked at him without speaking. He nodded to her and she nodded back. The meeting got loud very quickly; with forty-odd people crammed into a six-hundred-square-foot room, even whispered conversations created enough noise to fill the space completely.

He later recalled that, after that day, he found no immediate opportunities to speak to #47 at their monthly meetings. Too many people had issues to discuss, suggestions to make, or conflicts they needed him to resolve.

Had anyone asked him if he had envisioned that the project would grow to this magnitude back when he was training #2, #3, and #4, he would have been lying if he said he had. Yet by the time #2 introduced him to #13 and asked if he could bring this kid into the fold as well, he could sense that things would develop a bit differently than he had imagined. He never intended to assume control of any part of it, but maintained a totally hands-off attitude, much like this new way of living he had pioneered for the rest of them.

When attendance at the monthly meetings began exceeding twenty people, suggestions were made that they should establish a few professional guidelines before overwhelming numbers threatened the health of the venture. #6 had been the first to make this suggestion. #6 had been an administrator before his company fired him. He had already implored him several times in private to establish a few basic rules, otherwise chaos would be inevitable. #6 himself had been a victim of just such a circumstance at his old company.

In his heart, he despised all so-called rules, authority, and grid-lined organizational schemes, now even more intensely than before. But more and more people were showing up to meetings, and the majority of individuals were truly unfamiliar to him. It had occurred to him that, if he continued operating by trust and intuition alone, situations might arise that threatened his or others' way of life. So, in subsequent meetings he publicized a handful of basic guidelines, such as: someone who had "worked" a place or event could not do so more than once per year (especially important for banquets and meetings); members should not take jobs from those who were as badly off as they; if two or more members encountered each other at the same site, those arriving last should leave immediately; no one could reveal any information about the group or its members to outsiders; only those who had been members for over a year could develop new talent; internal conflict and external threat must be resolved through collective discussion at the monthly meeting, and so on.

A new order appeared more quickly than he had expected. Everyone studiously obeyed the new rules, while some went so far as to suggest, both in public and in private, that he continue to append new ones. Rules made people feel safe, he realized. Even people who had left the established track of "normal life" to forge their own path needed rules and a system to maintain inner stability.

A few people left; even more people joined in. Those who

left each had their own reasons. Some encountered positions that "truly fit them" and decided to stay put. Some who were getting married or starting families faced pressure from their spouse and chose to return to the numberless ranks of the unemployed. In his eyes, all of their reasons boiled down to fear of the lifestyle.

He gradually arrived at an indifferent acceptance of their comings and goings. He never thought himself capable of controlling other people's lives or choices. All he could do was present them with another undiscovered option.

He assumed after his first interaction with #47 that that would be it between the two of them. After #23, he just hadn't had the time to acquaint himself personally with every individual member, especially those who had been trained by other people. Most of the time, he only met them once, and it was entirely a matter of chance whether or not they ever spoke again. Yet to his surprise, a series of chance encounters allowed #47 to step into his world.

Even in his loneliest moments, he had never really felt the desire to partner up with anyone. There was no special personal reason for this, he had just never felt like it. Once over beers #2 had patted his shoulder and said it was probably the result of an unpleasant home life and a poor relationship between his parents. Yet he refused to accept such a formulaic analysis.

Just like they always say in romance novels, #47 really was different.

He ran into her a second time at a smaller get-together over dinner and drinks. As before, #5 had brought her along, and she was wearing the same light-blue skirt and graying canvas sneakers she had worn to the monthly meeting. That day she had just completed her first independent job, and the other guests made a show of toasting, congratulating, and welcoming her as an official member of the family.

Observing her closely, he watched her expression shift between discomfiture, enjoyment, and bashfulness. Yet whenever she looked at him, her gaze held a question. After they got together, he told her that it was that look of uncertainty that had attracted him from the outset.

It was curiosity. She was curious about him. Falling for someone is an easy thing to do, especially for people prone to feeling lonely. Any random reason can suffice to make two people attracted to each other. And his strongest desire was to find someone who made him curious and was equally as interested in him.

During the day, they each went off to work. In the evenings, as long as the weather wasn't horrifyingly cold, he liked holding her hand as they walked the streets. Whenever they passed a familiar place, he would tell her weird or miraculous stories about the "work" he'd done there, or she'd tell her stories to him. Day after day, they floated by like two molecules of smog in this city's densely polluted air, totally invisible and everywhere at once.

The intense, genuine interest that they had in each other, which inspired both to explore the other's emotional world, led him quickly to the discovery that she did not fully accept their way of life. What was more, her suspicion of it and resistance to it were growing by the day. At first, those feelings emerged only in the subtlest of responses—facial expressions, small movements, unconscious physical reactions. Later, she became less proactive about going out "gate-crashing" (their industry slang for looking for work), or she would simply spend the day wandering aimlessly, ignoring opportunities. While his compensation alone was more than enough to support two people, he saw very clearly that this thing of theirs had an expiration date.

She finally came to understand her own mind on one of that city's rarest days—a comfortable autumn evening. He was holding her hand as they leaned against a railing outside a café on the first floor of a large office building. He was telling her the story of a chance encounter he'd once had here.

"I kept my eye on the girl sitting alone in there for a good while. At first, she was holding her phone in a death grip and constantly looking around the café. She got more impatient the longer she waited and then, after even more waiting, her impatience disappeared. The disappointment in her eyes, that unspeakable embarrassment was painful to see. I walked up to her and smiled, and she immediately invited me to sit down across from her." He pointed into the café to show #47 where they had been sitting.

#47 nodded, her gaze unsteady, as if she were listening intently and emotionally absent at the same time.

"She talked to me for a long time—two hours or more, I'm guessing. She even treated me to a good lunch and a cup of coffee. She told me about her job, what movies she liked, her favorite desserts, how her relatives took turns pressuring her to meet people, and how her mother finally laid down the law and told her not to come home alone for New Year's. I listened and made harmless comments when I had to. I felt like there was nothing I could do to comfort her, nothing at all. Even if I really were willing to go out with her, be her boyfriend, go home with her for New Year's—even if I married her, I still wouldn't be able to bring her comfort."

Hearing this, she recovered herself and turned to look at him. There it was again, there it was—that look of curiosity or uncertainty in her eyes. He turned his head back toward the café and kept talking.

"Eventually the time came when she had to leave for something else, and she said goodbye and made to go. I'm almost never this impulsive, but I just couldn't resist: right as she was about to stand, I told her I wasn't actually the person she was waiting for. To my surprise she smiled and said yeah, she knew. For a second I was shocked, but when I recovered, I still felt this sort of laughable desire to try and comfort her one last time. The guy who never showed up, I said to her, missing out on you really was his loss. I couldn't believe my excitement would lead me to think of such a sentimental, bullshit line. She smiled again and said: Who said it wasn't?"

"Do you really think there's a future in this?" #47 suddenly blurted out an unrelated question, then slowly withdrew her hand from his.

"Well, here's the interesting part: Even as she put on her jacket and got ready to leave, I could sense that she had something she wanted to say to me, but she was vacillating and didn't dare open her mouth. In the end, after she'd put on her jacket, picked up her bag, and had no further reason to stick around, she asked me in a stuttering voice: 'Are...are you one of those?' At first, I didn't know how to reply; I had to look closely at her eyes before I figured out that she had spent the last two and a half hours thinking I was a sex worker. But it makes sense when you think about it. Who else would stop what they were doing for no reason just to sit down with a random girl and chat for hours on end?"

"I know you like living this way. But I just...I've had to think about this a lot lately. I mean, after my mother and father worked so hard to put me through four years of college—even if it wasn't a good school—does it really make sense for me to be doing something like this right after I graduated?"

He reached a warm and slightly sweaty hand toward her. She recoiled slightly; he drew his hand back.

"No one really cares about anyone else in this city. No one. Really. Cares. Eventually, you stop caring yourself." He covered his moist, warm right hand with an equally moist left hand.

"Often when you say things like this, they fascinate me. But in reality, I don't actually understand what you mean by them. Just like these things we're doing right now. And honestly, I don't see what's so interesting about turning into a person you originally weren't. It's not even a real transformation, it's just a performance." She exhaled deeply, as if rewarding herself for elucidating her thoughts clearly. "Can you tell me what exactly it is you plan to do? What kind of result this is supposed to produce?"

A weird, fuzzy sensation overtook him, as if a horde of this city's common fall caterpillars were crawling up his legs. He suddenly sensed that, from this moment, their relationship had nothing to do with romance; they were simply #1 and #47.

"I don't particularly plan to do anything, and I don't imagine there will be any concrete results. There are too many bugs in this city's program. The bigger bugs may be so big that people like us can only throw up our hands and cry, but the small ones can be fixed and reinstalled by hand, can't they? I want to reconfigure this unreasonable world by hand. That's what I want. It's a sort of new justice for people like me."

#47 reached out and politely pressed his left hand. Then she stood up and walked away.

He knew that when he got home he would find that #47 had cleaned up her things and moved out. Starting tomorrow, she would begin once more to look for a stable job, go on dates, get married, have kids, and burn her youth and life for this city that had absolutely no need for her.

Yet this was no longer the focus of his attention. Some ideas can exist without a body for as long as you do not force yourself to summarize them in coherent language. Yet in the very instant—it could be at any moment, in any environment—that you endow them with a concrete form, they immediately translate themselves into the substance of your spirit.

Thinking about what he had just said, he realized that this was just such a moment.

Yes—reconfigure by hand. Yes—people like me, a new justice. Yes, yes, yes.

A brand-new sense of purpose drove him to look at everything in a different light. His team grew at two or three times its original pace, spreading silently like water.

All talk of "position" was nothing but lies. It was and always had been a vast scam to make people willingly put themselves into spaces where they did not belong. Those people who were needed didn't care at all about the desires of others. So why shouldn't the people who weren't needed step in and reconfigure it all on their own?

"Most people come here in order to live. But I feel like I'm going to be here till I die." The phrase occasionally reappeared in his mind. Still no idea as to where he first read it, but by now the words had taken on new color. At its best, this sentence he had read somewhere in a book was only a beginning. It was up to him to write what came after. As for how it would end—well, guess we'll have to wait and see.

His people filled every corner of the city, opening new borders for it yet also pacifying it.

He wended his way through every shopping mall, down every street, and between every skyscraper, sometimes running into members of his team. No one ever stopped or greeted each other—just a nod, and both went about their business, conscious of an unspoken compact.

This secrecy made him happy.

Flourishing Beasts

荣华兽

Yan Ge

Translated by Jeremy Tiang

不是的。但再无后语。她是兽。喉咙中发出嘶吼。

"I waited for her to say more, but there was no more. She was a beast. Instead of words, a low growl rumbled in her throat."

All flourishing beasts are female. They live in herds and are placid by nature. Having green thumbs, they have made a living as gardeners since ancient times and are particularly skilled at raising rare species. A corruption of the word *flower* gives rise to their name, *flourishing*.

The flourishing beasts live in the southeastern corner of Yong'an City, at the Temple of the Antiquities. There, they grow all manner of plants in the back courtyard, filling it with fragrance all year round. The temple's flourishing Buddha is especially puissant for people seeking sons or mates, and so it receives a constant stream of incense offerings.

The flourishing beasts have delicate features etched with a perpetually worried look. They seldom speak. Their pale skin is marked with pale-blue crescent moons, and they have six fingers on each hand, but otherwise they are no different from any human woman. Their markings grow more vivid with age, turning first dark blue, then black. After this comes death. When a flourishing beast's life ends, her tribe cuts her into eight pieces, plants them, and waters the ground with yellow rice wine. A month later, a flourishing stem appears, flawlessly white, firm and lustrous as jade. After a month, this stem sprouts four limbs and, another month later, a face. Now beast-shaped, the wood continues to soften. One more month and the stem snaps off, and a new flourishing beast is born.

A young beast does not speak any human languages. She feasts on pollen and continues imbibing rice wine. After six months, she's the size of a three-year-old, with the features of a young woman. At this point, her words flow freely, and she brims with intelligence.

It is hard for flourishing beasts to reproduce. Of every eight pieces that are planted, only one or two survive. Conditions need to be exactly right, and they are particularly vulnerable during their embryonic stage, when human merchants are wont to chop them down for their high-quality wood, which is manufactured into small, exquisite household objects and sold for astronomical prices.

After the conflict in Yong'an City ended and a new government was installed, they brought in strict new laws prohibiting this practice, but the profits were just too enticing, and flourishing wood continued to be chopped down.

Flourishing beasts are peaceful and benevolent by nature. When the women of Yong'an have nowhere else to go, they retreat to the Temple of the Antiquities. There, they tend to the plants, or take care of the sprouting beasts and cubs. All live in harmony there, with everything they need.

These beasts live on honey, rice wine, eggs, and cauliflower. They eat no meat at all, being born to take holy orders.

*

One day in March, Zhong Liang came to visit me with a large box of instant noodles. Chuckling, he set it down. "A gift for you."

I looked sidelong at it, annoyed. "Zhong Liang, are you trying to murder your elders? There's got to be enough preservatives here to stuff a mummy."

He laughed some more. "I deserved that. All right, tell me what you like to eat, and I'll bring you that instead."

"Forget it," I said. "What do you want?"

He scratched his head. "There's a family gathering at my uncle's house next week. I'd like you to come with me."

"Why would you want me to come to a family gathering? Are you asking me to be your girlfriend?"

He looked as if he'd just stepped on a land mine. "I wouldn't dare," he said, which meant, "You're too old for me."

"My uncle likes your stories," he said. "When he found out

we were friends, he told me to invite you."

Ah, a fan. "No way." I never agreed to these kinds of requests.

The boy had a trick up his sleeve, though. He brought his handsome face close to mine and said, "The professor might be there. Will you come?"

"Sure," I blurted out.

Chagrined at having been so easily lured into revealing myself, I didn't say anything else, just shoved him out of my apartment.

"I'll pick you up at six next Friday!" called Zhong Liang as I closed the door on him.

*

By the time Friday rolled around, I'd completely forgotten about this. I was lounging in front of the TV eating ice cream in an oversized shirt, tousled and unwashed. When Zhong Liang knocked on the door and I opened it, we looked at each other in shock. "What the hell are you wearing?" we chorused.

He was all dressed up in a proper suit, back straight and expression solemn. Were we going to a funeral?

I remembered then about the gathering and, without even stopping to apologize, rushed into my bedroom. Five minutes later, I was back out, a pair of trousers beneath the shirt, my hair scraped back into a ponytail. That was the best I could do. "Let's go," I said.

Zhong Liang stared at me with a strange expression and studied me for a full three seconds before his face twitched and he said, "Fine."

*

Half an hour later, Zhong Liang's Fiat was pulling into the city's richest district, and I had an inkling that I was in trouble. He turned into the broad courtyard of his uncle's house, and I knew I'd been tricked.

That's how I ended up sitting across from the city's most famous jeweler, Zhong Ren. His nails were perfectly manicured as he took my hand, his grip firm and powerful. "Hello," he said.

I smiled foolishly. An empty smile. "Hello," I replied. Inwardly, I cursed Zhong Liang a thousand times. Why call this a *gathering*, when I was meeting him one-on-one?

Like a fish laid out on a slab, I was there for my reader, Mr. Zhong Ren, to examine. Zhong Liang sat in the window seat with a thick book in his hands, leaving us in the living room, facing each other like the two sides in a cold war negotiation.

"I like your stories," Zhong Ren said.

"So kind of you." All I could do was repeat the lines I'd used thousands of times before.

"I've read everything you've written about beasts," he said. "You make it all sound so real. The beasts are more human than the humans, and the humans are beastlier than the beasts."

I sipped my tea and smiled blankly. "It's not really so clear-cut."

We fell silent.

The man across from me looked kindly, as if he were my big brother, and his features were a little like Zhong Liang's. Something about his expression, though, made me think he had the sort of unease only young people feel. He was staring straight at me, from my forehead to my chin, then back up.

I felt goosebumps rising all over my skin. Finally, I said, "Mr. Zhong, I should really—"

"Let's get married," he said, as if startled from a dream.

He sounded sincere. I choked. The book fell from Zhong Liang's hand and thudded to the ground. *Damn you, so you were eavesdropping*. For some reason, that was the first thing to pop into my head.

*

It's not that difficult to avoid a person, but avoiding an over-eager, weirdly obstinate rich person is a little harder. I kept my head down for the next week, but he managed to track me down even somewhere as chaotic as the Dolphin Bar, his besotted face suddenly appearing before me and insisting, "Just hear me out." I lost all hope and wished that the glass in my hand contained not beer but arsenic.

I phoned Zhong Liang to shout at him, shaking all over, "This is all your fault, you bastard. You're not getting away with this."

Zhong Liang sounded stricken too. "Listen, my uncle's always been strange, but I hadn't realized how crazy he was. To think a woman like you could catch his eye—"

I shrieked and hung up. Taking deep breaths, I told myself: Don't get into a fight with a child, it's not worth it, he doesn't know how to appreciate an older...

I sat with the lights off waiting for his call. With Zhong Liang no doubt constantly broadcasting my location, there was no way he wouldn't know where I was. And yet, silence. All night long, the darkness pressed down on my head.

Finally, I couldn't stand it anymore. I picked up the phone and dialed.

"Hello?" Perfectly nonchalant.

I tried to speak, but my courage failed me and I hung up. Trying to pretend nothing had happened, I burst into tears.

My mother used to say: never cry, or your tears will water your sorrow and it'll grow.

Finally, I picked up the phone and called another number.

As soon as I said "hello," Chen Nian knew who I was.

"What's wrong?" she said. "Are you unhappy?"

"Yes," I said. "I want to come and stay for a while."

"Come," said Chen Nian.

*

"My mother once told me, 'Don't bother Chen Nian unless you're at the end of your rope. I've already given her enough trouble.'"

"Don't be silly," said Chen Nian. "It's been ten years, and I still miss her a lot."

She sat next to me sipping her tea. Her hair was loose, just washed. It looked beautifully soft and glossy in the sunlight. A soothing scent hung in the air. I recognized it right away, from all the time I'd spent here as a child with my mother: incense from the burners, plants in the back garden, various birds and insects, as well as the damp, woody fragrance of Chen Nian herself.

As ever, there was suffering in her face. She was old now, and since the last time I'd seen her, the markings on her body had turned a deep blue, the skin translucently thin over them and seemingly empty inside. She gently placed her hand on mine. "Don't worry, of course you can stay here. Shall we put you in your mother's old room?"

I nodded yes, and took a deep breath. My spirit settled as I clasped her hand. Her six fingers were ice-cold.

She was a flourishing beast, and this was the Temple of the Antiquities. Finally, my heart was at rest.

*

A young beast took me to the guest room in the back courtyard. Her neck was long and elegant, and her pale-blue markings were like butterflies beneath her skin. "You can call me Zhu Huai," she said, smiling. She must have been around ten, which meant she looked like a twenty-year-old human. Her voice was delicate and crisp. I'd never seen her before.

She seemed shy and scurried off after saying she'd come fetch me for dinner.

Nothing about the room had changed, apart from the TV set that now stood in a corner, and the enormous electric fan suspended from the ceiling.

I sat on the sofa and looked out the window. The rear courtyard was as verdant as ever. Flowers I didn't know the names of bloomed in all sorts of unimaginable colors. The only ones I could identify were plum blossoms, swathes of them in pale pink and white. My mother once said, "I love these more than buying a real silk dress from Tianmei Mall."

I smiled.

That night, Chen Nian made me tofu stew. A unfamiliar aroma rose from it, instantly appetizing. We had it with rice. The fluorescent lights in the great hall burned steadily, and the news was showing on the wall-mounted plasma TV. Chen Nian pointed at a gaggle of beasts sitting to our left and said they were all born after I'd left. I turned to look and saw the young beast from earlier smiling right back at me. She had a refined beauty, and her eyes were as I remembered, moist and alluring. Chen Nian said, "You've met Zhu Huai?"

"Yes."

"She likes you."

I smiled. "I like her too."

At the other end of the great hall, a group of human women sat at a round table, eating the meat dishes that had been laid out for them. They looked even more sorrowful than the flourishing beasts, whose faces were naturally etched with suffering. Their hair was dyed all sorts of peculiar hues. All of a sudden, one of them threw down her chopsticks, buried her face in her hands, and burst into loud sobs.

Chen Nian shook her head. "Times have changed. Everyone likes to cry these days."

The local news ended, and Zhong Ren's face appeared on the screen. He said my name. "Where are you? I can't find you. Please come back quickly, I need to talk to you."

Chen Nian grinned slyly at me.

My appetite vanished.

That night, though, I slept very soundly and dreamed of my mother, young but with pure-white hair. Sitting in the window seat, she listened to a staticky radio, singing quietly along.

Her voice was faint and turned into moans of pain, as if ants were nibbling at her entrails. Each cry stabbed into my ears.

I woke up to find the sun high in the sky. I was covered in sweat.

*

I opened the door and saw the flourishing beasts outside, all dressed in white, heads bowed beneath the gorgeous flowering plum tree. They were mumbling a chant.

The young beasts were standing at the back, holding hands. I thought I saw them trembling. From the far end, Zhu Huai turned and saw me. There were tears in her eyes, and somehow she looked like my mother.

Over lunch, I asked Chen Nian what had happened, and she told me a flourishing tree had been cut down.

An old beast had died that January and, as usual, had been planted in eight segments, three of which sprouted. One of these had just been chopped down and stolen.

Zhu Huai took me to see the two surviving saplings. They

looked lonely beneath the flowering plum tree. We could only stare at them from a distance. A face and markings were faintly visible on each.

Their limbs were just coming in, plump and stubby, like a baby's.

"Beautiful," I sighed.

Zhu Huai turned to face me. She had an eye-catching crescent-moon mark right across her left cheek, and her expression was sorrowful. "It's not," she said.

I waited for her to say more, but there was no more. She was a beast. Instead of words, a low growl rumbled in her throat.

*

The flourishing beasts at the Temple of the Antiquities were split into two groups: the older ones tended to the temple, while the younglings looked after the plants in the rear garden. Zhu Huai and I were in charge of the flowering plum. "Each of us is assigned to a plant," she explained, "and mine is this tree." Her eyes were full of love, and although she was just a young beast, there was something motherly about her as she watered, fertilized, and pruned. She stroked the bark tenderly and said, "Look, there was an infestation when I was four. It left behind these scars, poor thing."

"You must have been scolded for that," I said. "What kind of flourishing beast can't look after a tree?"

She laughed. "It's not like that. Even with flourishing beasts taking care of them, trees will get attacked by bugs, they'll rot away, they'll die. It's a law of nature. That's all we get in this life, and all we can hope for is that we leave behind some good seeds."

I patted her head. "So young, and already you sound like an old woman." My mother used to say these words to me too.

I was a little girl then. She'd taken me to pray to the flourishing Buddha, and I'd looked up and realized the white jade he was carved from was actually beast wood, pale and flawless.

My mother said perhaps they'd done this in remembrance of the beasts who'd been cut down for their wood. The murdered beasts.

Zhu Huai and I swept the courtyard together. When we were done, she said she wanted to watch TV—there was a new series she was crazy about. It happened to be one that an old friend and I had laughed over. I sat with her, trying to be patient, waiting for the commercial break so I could relieve my eyes with breast enhancement ads instead of this rubbish.

Instead, though, it was Zhong Ren's face that appeared on the screen. His chin was covered in stubble, and he looked unwell. "Where are you?" he said. "Come back soon. I have so much to say to you. Please marry me."

Zhu Huai thought this was a trailer for a new series and looked excited about it, while I tried not to vomit. How could a man who'd done so well in business, with so much money in the bank, be such a blockhead? He was scouring the world for me, while the person I actually longed to see remained completely silent.

I sighed.

In the end, I couldn't stand it any longer and turned on my cellphone for the first time in days. Right away, I was almost deafened by the chorus of notifications. Most of the messages were from Zhong Ren, each one using almost the same words. I deleted them as quickly as I could.

There were a few from Zhong Liang too. "You've hidden yourself really well. Please come back. My uncle is tearing our family apart."

Just as I was thinking, *serves you right*, the phone rang. An unknown number.

I hesitated before answering. "Hello?" Silence. "Hello?" Call ended.

That must be him. As soon as he knew I was all right, he'd hung up, no doubt so he could curse my ancestors eighteen generations back. I burst out laughing.

Let him curse me. How much longer would this go on for? Back in the lab, the slightest mistake in an experiment used to get me such a scolding I wouldn't be able to eat for three days. He scolded me if my assignments were imperfect, or if I got anything wrong in an exam. When I dropped out of school, he'd stared at me with such hatred, I thought he'd have dug out my heart if he could.

I laughed again at the thought and shook my head.

*

Chen Nian summoned me for afternoon tea. She'd dug out a photograph of herself with my mother to show me. She'd just been a young girl then and looked the same age as me now. Flourishing beasts are so short-lived. Like grass, they begin withering at the age of one.

In the picture, she was smiling so broadly that her natural expression of suffering was all but invisible. She and my mother were holding hands, standing in the rear courtyard.

Now she was old and crinkled all over. I could hear her bones rubbing together when she walked. Her skin came off in flakes, and the markings beneath it were almost black, like tiny bottomless holes.

She said she had a surprise for me. She looked in pain, like someone in the final stages of a disease.

It was an album, highly decorated, full of photographs of white furniture.

Each of these had been made from a murdered flourishing beast. Those whose limbs had just sprouted were still hard and could be turned into tables. Those whose faces had started showing were softer and could provide natural cushioning when made into chairs. Others were cabinets, sliced into thin segments or ornamentally carved. Regardless, every one of them was white as snow, without the slightest flaw.

"Aren't they beautiful?"

"Yes," I said, and I meant it. The flourishing beasts were so beautiful that their corpses couldn't be allowed to remain whole.

Chen Nian kept turning the pages, and there was admiration in her eyes. Such beauty.

Chairs, tables, cupboards, sculptures, doors, all sorts of objects. The most striking were the ones with faces, their eyes half-open. They looked like living things. Clean, classical lines or flowing, modern curves. "Every murdered beast is in here," said Chen Nian.

She closed the album and dropped it on the table with a thud. It sat there, thick as an encyclopedia.

"I've read your stories." She took a sip of tea. "You should write about us too."

I had to choke back a sob. "I will," I said.

*

That night at dinner, I kept my head bent over my food, for fear of seeing Zhong Ren's face on the TV screen. He didn't show up, and Chen Nian smiled at me as I let out a sigh of relief. Thank god he'd finally given up.

Zhu Huai noticed my expression and leaned toward me. "What's wrong?"

"She's just happy," said Chen Nian. "Now she can leave this awful place. She can go drinking and start partying again."

Zhu Huai stared at me. "You're leaving?" Tears began to roll down her cheeks.

Chen Nian pulled the young beast into her arms and soothed her, staring all the while at me, brow crinkled. "So rude of her. After living alongside human women for too long, our children learn to cry too."

I blushed and pasted a vacant smile on my face.

Chen Nian patted Zhu Huai on the head. "I don't blame you for not wanting her to go. Back when you were just a sapling, it was her mother who tended you." She stroked the young beast's face. "You spent so much time together, you even look like her. She tended all of you so carefully, back then. What a shame you were the only one who survived."

I froze, my eyes fixed on the little beast. She stared back at me, eyes glimmering with tears. My mother's face.

And just like that, a trail of cold sweat trickled down my spine.

*

I couldn't get to sleep that night. I sat sprawled against the window, gazing at the shadowy outlines of the courtyard greenery. In the distance, the glow of the city swept the sky like searchlights. The only thing I could see clearly was the flowering plum by the beds where the beast saplings grew. My mother had planted this tree with her own hands. Chen Nian had been there too and said to her, "I'll take care of this for you."

My mother died in this temple, and the plum tree still stands tall.

Out of nowhere, I heard sobbing, and then an anguished howl, like an injured wild animal. My palms prickled with sweat. Another scream.

This was no hallucination. They were coming thicker now, those cries and moans, like a chorus of chanted scripture, filling the air around me.

The loudest shrieks were coming from Chen Nian's room.

I jumped out of bed and ran over there barefoot. The flourishing beasts were huddled outside her door, all dressed in white, the blue markings on their skin glowing in the dark through their clothes. I heard Chen Nian yowling in pain, her voice shredded.

I strode through the throng of beasts, who didn't seem to notice me. They knelt there, shaking all over, letting out a keening wail.

As soon as I saw her, I knew. Chen Nian was dying.

She lay in bed, eyes sunken and hollow. Cry after cry came from her throat. Her body was covered in gleaming black markings, and her skin was completely transparent, peeling away. Plump worms, about the size of my thumb, were wriggling from the cracks. They were snow white and perfectly smooth, crawling slowly over her body.

Flourishing beasts stood around her, holding down her writhing body, tears pouring down their faces.

I took this all in, then ran out into the courtyard, where I bent over and threw up.

*

I left the Temple of the Antiquities the next morning. Zhu Huai saw me out, her face pale as she walked behind me, as if nothing had happened. We were silent as we passed through the rear courtyard to the great hall and then out.

She hesitated, then reached out to take my hand. "Chen Nian died yesterday."

"I know," I said. Her six-fingered hand was cold as ice, and the blue markings on her wrist looked darker than I remembered. Involuntarily, I recoiled as if from an electric shock and stepped through the door, brushing past a pious pilgrim. When I turned back, I saw the pure-white flourishing Buddha, like a tree rising to the heavens.

Zhu Huai was smiling grimly at me. "Goodbye," she said.

I took a taxi home. The sun was bright on this late spring day, and I felt as if I were finally awakening from a nightmare.

That feeling lasted till I got to my front door, where Zhong Liang was crouched like a plainclothes detective, or really more like a human trafficker. He had panda-like dark circles beneath his eyes, and he was sucking on a cigarette. The ground around him was littered with butts. I turned and ran as if I'd seen a ghost, but he was too fast for me. In a few seconds, he'd caught up and grabbed hold of me.

"Let me go," I yelled. "I need to sleep. Your uncle's finally leaving me alone, don't tell me you've gone mad too."

"My uncle's dead," he said.

His mouth was right by my ear, and I felt his hot breath on my icy cheek.

*

Zhong Liang dragged me along to the funeral. As befitted

a famous jeweler, the room was as heavily ornamented as a palace, and streams of people came and went nonstop. I was yellow and shriveled like old celery. Zhong Liang made me stand in front of his uncle's black-and-white photo-graph. Zhong Ren looked like a successful man, the sort who goes around breezily setting the world straight. He was handsome, I realized, with a scholar's good looks. I bowed deeply to him three times.

Zhong Ren's sister received me with the hauteur of a queen. "So you're the girl my little brother spent all that time chasing after." She squinted at me, and I just stood there enduring her scrutiny. Finally, she sighed, "It's a shame he never married..."

My scalp prickled. Was she trying to talk me into a ghost wedding? Fortunately, she said instead, "My brother left you something. I'll send Zhong Liang to get it." I rejoiced—how lucky that modern society had left behind superstitions like forcing women to betroth themselves to dead men.

Zhong Liang brought me to claim Zhong Ren's bequest to me. I protested all the while that I barely knew the man, I wasn't family, I'd done nothing to deserve this, I couldn't just take a handout... But he said nothing, just strode ahead with a dark expression, and I lapsed into silence.

We arrived at Zhong Ren's house. Because the property was being sold, most of the furniture had already been moved out, and it looked much more spacious than when I'd seen it before. Zhong Liang told me to take a seat in the living room while he went inside. He emerged with a large box. "Take this," he said.

The cardboard box was for a 29-inch color television, but I wasn't naïve enough to think Zhong Ren had left me a TV set. "What is it?" I stammered.

How the mighty had fallen—not long ago, this young man had smiled radiantly and addressed me with respect. And now, he might as well have been a zombie as he stared at me, face blank, and said, "A chair."

A chair.

He was enough of a gentleman not to make me carry the box home all by myself, but the second we got it through my front door, he vanished as if fleeing a plague house.

Finally, I could lounge on my comfortable sofa. The first thing I did was get some ice cream from the freezer. Fortunately, it was still before the expiration date.

I stared at the box as I ate from the carton, but I couldn't be bothered to open it. Why had this bizarre man given me a chair, after forcing me to flee my own home? I'd rather he'd been more like his nephew and left me a crate of instant noodles.

Why a chair?

A thought struck me and I put down the ice cream. The squat, square box cast a dark shadow.

What kind of chair?

I got a pair of scissors and cut the tape, shaking all over.

A snow-white chair.

It was classically designed, of a style fashionable over ten years ago, pure white all over, made of a softly yielding material. Even an idiot could have guessed it cost a fortune. An intricate carving decorated its back, in the middle of which was the faint impression of a woman's face, her eyes half shut. She could have been my twin.

I stared at her. She seemed to sense me, and her eyes opened wide. She looked back at me, smiling.

I shrieked as my legs gave way under me.

*

I drank a glass of hot milk, scalding my tongue. Finally, the sense of unreality faded, and I came back to myself. When I looked again, it was clear: this was a flourishing beast who'd been turned into a chair after her untimely death, one of the eight that my mother had tended. A cozy chair with pleasantly rounded edges. Zhong Ren had touched every inch of her. Ten years ago, he'd liked her at first sight, and so he had acquired her. Every day, in his vast house, he stroked her and spoke to her, finally coming to love her.

I shut my eyes and touched the dead beast's face. I thought I could still feel the warmth of his hand.

When Zhong Ren asked me to marry him, I darted away like a startled bird. Now he was dead, and I could finally cry about it.

My mother died long ago, but hell does not exist in Yong'an City, and so the souls of the deceased drift aimlessly across the land instead.

I wished I could believe that Chen Nian's soul would meet my mother's beneath the flowering plum tree, while Zhong Ren's could take this beast's hand and warm her six ice-cold fingers with his breath.

Night in the city is as bright as day. Light seeped in through the window, burnishing the chair.

My tears plopped crisply onto the floor.

I called my professor. "Hello," he said.

"I've come back."

"Are you better?"

"Yes, much better."

Silence. We were both stubborn, and so insignificant. A standoff.

Finally, I said, "I miss you very much."

He seemed startled, and it took him a long time to say, "Yes, me too."

*

I sat down to write the story of the flourishing beasts, narrated by one of them. "I died before I was born," I had her say. "I was hacked into pieces and turned into a chair. My limbs were ripped apart, my entrails mutilated. One day, a man bought me for a lot of money. Because he wanted me. He placed me by his bed but couldn't bear to sit on me, so instead he gazed at me and talked, touching my face and kissing me. My heart was still tender."

There was a plum tree in the park too, but its blossoms had long ago fallen. It was so hot. The girls at the Dolphin Bar wore less and less, and the number of one-night stands increased.

I published my flourishing beasts story: a lingering love affair, a weeping girl praying at the Temple of the Antiquities.

I had to smile. Everyone was intoxicated, and life passed like a wisp of smoke.

Nothing in life ever stays unchanged. One day, Zhong Liang came to find me at the Dolphin Bar.

"I shouldn't have blamed you," he said. "Everyone has their own fate. I know that now."

I bought him a drink; he held his liquor well. I could have made a bad boy out of him—but then would I get in trouble with my professor?

We were plastered by the time I called him a taxi. He flung his arms around my neck and refused to let go. I peeled them off and pushed him into the car, and even then he stuck his head out to call after me, like an overgrown child, "Please don't be angry with me, it's because my uncle died so horribly. His tongue was bitten clean off, so I—"

I was sober before he'd finished the sentence, and froze so suddenly that someone almost walked into me.

Back home, I used what was left of my Dutch courage to rip the chair apart. I picked up the backrest and broke the face right across my knee. Sure enough, there it was, a strip of red amongst the white: a human tongue. I tried to pull it out, but it was embedded so deep, as if the wood had absorbed it into itself. There was no way to retrieve it.

The beast had gotten jealous. She thought he'd fallen in love with someone else, and so she bit off his tongue the next time they kissed. That's why she smiled when she saw me. I hadn't imagined it.

*

Two days later, I got a package from the Temple of the Antiquities, with a note that read: "Chen Nian asked me to give you this." It was a wooden headrest, exquisitely carved with fluid lines, snow-white and ice-cold, yielding to the touch. An object of value. Right in the center, a woman's face was just visible, not one I recognized. Another suffering woman who'd once tended a sapling. The eyes were hooded, but when they looked at me, I could see Chen Nian in them.

I clutched the wooden block on my lap. The face smiled at me. Just a smile, no words.

*

Flourishing beasts are white as snow, and their wood is strong yet yielding, a sought-after commodity. However, the vast majority are infested with worms as saplings and grow up to be diseased creatures, covered in the blue marks of the pests devouring them from within. When the markings turn black, they die.

When a beast passes, the worms exit her body, which is then cut into eight pieces: head, chest, belly, four limbs, heart. These are buried in the soil, in the hope of further life.

When a beast manages to avoid the predations of worms, the entire community rejoices and chops it down to make furniture. This is the true calling of flourishing beasts, and in this form they can live for thousands of years. Such beasts will never speak again, but they will live in comfort and ease, their hearts at rest.

As for the worm-ridden unfortunates who will never be

whole, they must live as diseased beasts, spending their days eating vegetarian and chanting scriptures, praying to the flourishing Buddha to be liberated from this sea of troubles as early as possible. They adore all wood, even envy it.

Flourishing beasts are placid by nature and dislike movement. Like a wild meadow that withers and blooms, they enact the cycle of nature, rising like a phoenix from its ashes. Only a very few ever attain their true form.

And yet the flourishing beasts remain at peace, for this is not their plight alone but the fate of every living thing.

Authors

Chan Chi Wa, born in Hong Kong, is a freelance writer, editor, and film critic. He was the president of the Hong Kong Film Critics Society from 2012 to 2015 and editor of the literary magazine *Fleurs des lettres* from 2007 to 2011. His short story collection, The elephant that vanished, was published in 2008.

Chen Si'an is a playwright, theater director, poet, short story writer, and literary translator. She was born in Inner Mongolia and now lives and works in Beijing. She has published three collections of short stories and six plays. Her plays have been performed at the Royal Court Theatre, the Edinburgh International Festival, the National Theatre Company of China, and the Beijing International Fringe Festival. She is executive editor of Wings Poetry and founder of the international script-reading event Sound and Fury.

Enoch Tam has been writing for more than ten years and follows the practices of renowned Hong Kong authors Quanan, Xi Xi, Dung Kai-cheung, and Hon Lai-chu, and devotes his creativity to the combination of surrealist and magical realist city writings.

Dorothy Tse is an award-winning writer from Hong Kong. She has published three story collections in Chinese and one in English, *Snow and Shadow* (translated by Nicky Harman). She was cofounder of the *Fleurs des lettres* literary journal and currently teaches literature and creative writing at Hong Kong Baptist University.

Yan Ge was born in Sichuan, China. Her first short story collection was published in China when she was seventeen. She is the author of thirteen books, including six novels. She has received numerous awards, including the prestigious Mao Dun Literature Prize (Best Young Writer), and she was named by *People's Literature* magazine as one of twenty future literary masters in China. The English translation of her novel *The Chilli Bean Paste Clan* was published in 2018, and her novel *Strange Beasts of China*, translated by Jeremy Tiang, is forthcoming from Tilted Axis Press in 2020.

Zhu Hui was born in Jiangsu, China. He is editor-in-chief of the journal *Yu hua* and author of four novels and more than eighty short stories. His awards include the Wang Zengqi Award and the 2018 Lu Xun Literary Prize, China's most prestigious literary award.

Translators

Natascha Bruce translates fiction from Chinese. She has translated short stories by Dorothy Tse for BBC Radio 3, *Denver Quarterly*, *Words Without Borders*, *Wasafiri*, and others. Her book-length translations include *Lonely Face* by Yeng Pway Ngon, *A Classic Tragedy* by Xu Xiaobin (co-translated with Nicky Harman), and *Lake Like a Mirror* by Ho Sok Fong. She lives in Santiago, Chile.

Michael Day is a traveler, writer, and translator from Chinese and Japanese based in Mexico City, though originally from the American Midwest. His recent work has appeared in the *Los Angeles Review of Books China Channel*, *Chicago Quarterly Review*, *Structo*, *Saint Ann's Review*, and *Words Without Borders*. He was joint winner of the 2015 Bai Meigui Translation Prize for Chinese to English literary translation.

Audrey Heijns is a translator of Chinese poetry and prose, and the editor of *VerreTaal*, an online database of Chinese literature in Dutch translation found at unileiden.net/verretaal.

Canaan Morse is a literary translator and poet, currently pursuing a PhD in imperial Chinese literature at Harvard. His translations of poems by Yang Xiaobin, He Qifang, and several other poets have been published in *Kenyon Review*, *The Baffler*, *Asymptote*, and elsewhere. His translation of Ge Fei's novel *The Invisibility Cloak* (NYRB Classics Series) won the 2014 Susan Sontag Award for Translation. Cofounder of *Pathlight: New Chinese Writing*, he coedited the anthology *We Agree on Nothing: New Writing from China* and currently serves as editor-in-chief of Books from Taiwan.

Jeremy Tiang has translated novels by Li Er, Zhang Yueran, Yan Ge, Yeng Pway Ngon, Chan Ho-Kei, and Su Wei-chen, among others. He also writes and translates plays. His novel *State of Emergency* won the Singapore Literature Prize in 2018. He is a member of the literary translation collective Cedilla & Co. and the managing editor of *Pathlight* magazine.